'I don't feel pity for you, Crystal. And don't even attempt to tell me what I can and can't do!'

She blinked dazedly. 'But I wasn't—'

'Yes, you were. You—oh, to hell with it!' he exclaimed, before his head lowered and his mouth took fierce possession of hers.

Crys was so stunned by the unexpectedness of his actions that for a few brief moments she stood unmoving in the tight band of his arms, the slenderness of her body crushed against the hardness of his as he very thoroughly kissed her.

So thoroughly, in fact, that she felt a long-forgotten stirring of desire. Heat, like molten lava, moved slowly into her body, and it felt as if the ice in her heart was melting. As, indeed, it probably was, she realised with a choked cry. All warmth, all desire, had died with James. But this man, an admitted enigma, *couldn't* be the one to heal her battered emotions!

Carole Mortimer says: 'I was born in England, the youngest of three children—I have two older brothers. I started writing in 1978, and have now written over one hundred books for Mills & Boon®. I have four sons, Matthew, Joshua, Timothy and Peter, and a bearded collie called Merlyn. I'm very happily married to Peter senior; we're best friends as well as lovers, which is probably the best recipe for a successful relationship. We live on the Isle of Man.'

Recent titles by the same author:

KEEPING LUKE'S SECRET

The Bachelor Cousins trilogy
TO MARRY McCLOUD
TO MARRY McKENZIE
TO MARRY McALLISTER

AN ENIGMATIC MAN

BY

CAROLE MORTIMER

MILLS & BOON®

For Peter

First published in Great Britain 2003
Harlequin Mills & Boon Limited,
Eton House, 18-24 Paradise Road, Richmond, Surrey TW9 1SR

© Carole Mortimer 2003

ISBN 0 263 83231 7

Set in Times Roman 10½ on 12 pt.
01-0503-44563

Printed and bound in Spain
by Litografía Rosés, S.A., Barcelona

CHAPTER ONE

DRACULA'S castle!

No…on second thoughts, Crys decided, that was perhaps being a little unkind to Dracula!

She had been driving for hours, had stopped the car at the top of the driveway in the hopes of somehow getting her bearings in the rapidly deepening fog. But all such thoughts had fled as she saw the name of the house grooved into one of the stone pillars that flanked the broken-down gateway. Her startled gaze moved to the monstrosity of a house just visible at the end of the driveway. Victorian Gothic architecture—and every era since, if the numerous extensions were anything to go by.

The whole thing jarred on Crys's heightened sense of line and design.

This couldn't possibly be her destination—couldn't be the Yorkshire home of the elder brother of her good friend Molly. Molly was slightly eccentric, yes—a little unorthodox, too—but that was no reason to suppose it ran in the family!

Crys frowned up at the pillar closest to her. Despite the covering of moss, the name 'Falcon House' was still readable. She picked up the letter she had received from Molly several days ago, quickly scanning its contents until she came to the directions for finding Sam Barton's home. The name 'Falcon House' clearly stood out from Molly's otherwise hurried scrawl.

But this place wasn't really a house at all. It was a castle, with high turrets and towers, and even what looked like a defunct moat encircling the outer walls.

Perhaps Sam's home was at the back of this monstrosity? Hadn't Molly mentioned at some time that her brother was caretaking the place for an absent friend?

Having now seen Falcon House, Crys wasn't at all surprised the owner was absent most of the time—it would give anyone nightmares to actually have to live in this dilapidated old pile.

Yes, she decided, that had to be the answer. If she drove down the driveway and over the rickety-looking drawbridge, there was sure to be a smaller—more comfortable!—house situated somewhere at the back.

Except, as Crys discovered a few minutes later, having driven slowly down the rutted and holed road and into the forecourt to a castle encircled by a moat—albeit an empty, smelly old moat full of indescribable rubbish—there was virtually nothing behind the building. Just a small piece of land that probably should have been a garden but was so overgrown with bushes and trees it resembled a jungle!

Crys parked her car, climbing out onto moss-covered gravel and stretching her tired limbs even as she gazed up and up at the tumbledown castle before her, taking in the pipes that hung loose on the walls, the several tiles that had slid off the roof to lie shattered on the ground below.

Even through the damp fog Crys could see that most of the lower windows were either boarded up completely or had curtains drawn against prying eyes. The windows on the upper floors, although virtually all intact, seemed to look blankly out on the rest of the world.

Not exactly welcoming, and the whole place had such a neglected air that Crys was sure no one could actually be living in it. It—

She had heard something!

It was an undistinguishable, muted sound, but nevertheless she had heard a noise of some sort. It seemed to be coming from the side of the house.

She swallowed hard, hesitating. Should she go and investigate, and risk goodness knows what? Or should she simply get back in her car and drive quickly away?

The second choice definitely had its own appeal. But hadn't she spent the last year running away from one situation or another? Wasn't it time to stand her ground and face whatever it was that needed facing? Wasn't this exactly what her acceptance of Molly's invitation to spend some days in Yorkshire with her at the home of her brother had all been about?

There again, was this really the right occasion for her to start facing up to the world once again?

Crys almost laughed out loud at the ludicrousness of the situation she found herself in. Almost...

It had been a big step for her to accept Molly's invitation at all—to make the long and tiring journey from London to Yorkshire. Only to be confronted with—this.

But what was 'this', really? She'd turned into the drive of a dilapidated old castle, and the blinding fog was adding to its air of mystery and so increasing her unease, despite the fact that the property gave every indication of being uninhabited.

Except for a rhythmically grating sound coming from the side of the house…

Easily sorted, Crys told herself briskly. She would just have to go and investigate. If it was just the brisk wind blowing a branch against one of those sightless windows, fine. If the sound was a human being, she would simply ask for directions to Sam Barton's home and be on her way.

But her resolve was shaken somewhat when she passed under the archway that led onto the forecourt and found herself face to face with the largest dog she had ever seen in her life!

Crys gasped, coming to an abrupt halt as the dog bared its teeth and growled low in its throat, huge shoulders bunched in readiness as it prepared to leap at her.

Her mouth felt suddenly dry, every bone and muscle in her body tense with the shock of confrontation, wide gaze held in the hypnotic effect of those steely canine eyes.

And all the time the gigantic beast kept up that low growl that closely resembled the threat of thunder.

'What is it, Merlin?' prompted a disembodied voice.

If Crys had been rigid with shock before, she suddenly felt icy tentacles of fear gliding down her back. She had always wondered what was meant by a 'cold sweat'—now she knew!

Where had that voice come from? There was no one else here in this swirling fog but herself and this ferocious-looking dog, and yet she had definitely heard a voice. Male, she thought. Although it had been slightly muffled, so it was difficult to be sure.

What did it matter whether the voice had belonged

to a male or female—as long as it had been a *voice*! At the moment she felt very much in need of the presence of another human being.

If it had been human...

Get a grip, Crys, she instantly instructed herself impatiently. Okay, so it was creepy here, with the swirling fog surrounding her and that towering monstrosity behind her, and the Hound of the Baskervilles standing in front of her, barring her way, but that was no reason to simply give in to the panic and turn and run!

Yes, it was!

Any minute now this huge beast might tire of just growling and launch itself at her, huge jaws slavering as it ripped and tore at the delicate skin of her throat. She—

'I'm warning you now, Merlin, that if you follow any more rabbits down their holes I'm not coming after you and digging you out again.' The disembodied voice came hollowly through the fog a second time.

It *was* a man! He was somewhere close at hand too, Crys was sure. Close enough to save her from this wild dog, she hoped.

'Help!'

Wonderful—her lips were so numbed that the cry barely came out as a squeak! Although it was enough to turn that low rumbling growl into a full-throated warning of intent. The dog was clearly preparing to leap for her unprotected throat!

'Help!' Her second cry was louder. Loud enough to be heard, she prayed silently—because she really didn't hold out much hope for the dog's continued stillness!

'Damn it, Merlin, I— What on earth—? Down, Merlin,' the man called impatiently, and the dog's snarl instantly changed to a muted growl.

Crys's scream had cut across the man's initial remark as a head suddenly appeared out of the ground about ten feet away from her: a dark, shaggy head, with a beard of several days' growth covering the lower half of a face only alleviated by the fierceness of dark green eyes glittering brightly through the gloom of the fog.

But at least the dog had taken heed of his master, falling back on his haunches now, even its growling having come to a stop—although its gaze remained fixed on Crys's slightest move. Waiting, no doubt, for his master to give the order to attack!

But she had no intention of moving. She hadn't been able to do more than stare since that body had appeared out of the ground!

Maybe this was Dracula's castle, after all. Maybe—

Her eyes widened apprehensively as the man used a spade to lever himself easily out of what appeared to be a hole in the ground. A hole about six feet long, three feet wide, and she had no idea how deep…!

Her vision moved to the man's feet as he straightened, then travelled up the long length of his legs, in what appeared to be black denims, and over a broad chest and muscular arms in a thick black jumper. He had darkly waving hair growing long onto his shoulders, and of course the dark growth of beard that concealed his face. Except for those piercing green eyes.

The man seemed huge, several inches over six feet, the powerful force of his muscled body as tensed for action as his dog's had been seconds ago.

In fact, now that Crys could clearly see him, she wasn't sure if the dog wasn't a safer bet!

She moistened dry lips, willing herself to remain calm. 'Hello,' she managed huskily.

The hard mouth tilted sideways, hinting at the scorn with which the man welcomed her greeting. '"Hello"?' he returned scathingly.

Crys was still badly shaken, first from the encounter with the dog, and then the sudden appearance of this man almost as if from nowhere. But that didn't mean she was a complete quivering wreck!

'What were you doing in there?' She indicated the hole. It was January, so too late for digging the garden over, and also too early for planting out. Besides, from the size and depth of the hole…!

Dark brows rose over his glittering green eyes. 'What do you think I was doing?'

Despite his dishevelled state, the untidiness of his hair and growth of beard, the man had an educated voice. In fact under other circumstances it might have been quite a pleasant voice.

Under other circumstances…

Crys gave a slight shiver as she glanced over at the hole he appeared to have been digging. 'I have no idea,' she answered guardedly.

The man didn't actually appear to have moved, and yet somehow he suddenly looked tenser than ever, the spade in his hand slightly threatening. 'Take a guess,' he challenged hardly.

Crys swallowed hard. This was ridiculous. She simply wanted directions to Sam Barton's house, not to indulge in verbal games with a complete stranger. A dangerous-looking one, at that.

'Look, I'm really sorry to have bothered you—'

'You bother Merlin more than you do me,' the man dismissed coldly.

'Merlin...? Oh, you mean the dog,' she realised belatedly. The huge beast was sitting at its master's feet now, but still watching her every move. At the mention of his name he began that low growling once again...

The man gave a humourless smile. 'He isn't too keen on being called that.'

Crys blinked. 'But I thought you said Merlin was his name?' She frowned her puzzlement.

'It is.' The man nodded tersely. 'I was referring to your reference to his species.'

'But—'

'You and I both know what he is,' the man cut in impatiently. 'Merlin is the one who has doubts, and I think it better if we humour him—don't you?'

Crys glanced down at the slavering animal. 'Exactly what sort of...what breed is he?' she amended, opting on the side of caution. After all, Merlin had only just stopped growling again.

'Irish Wolfhound,' the man supplied. 'Now, I'm sure it's been very pleasant passing the time of day with you—' his tone implied otherwise '—but, as you can no doubt see, I have a grave to finish digging. So if you wouldn't mind—'

'It really is a grave?' she gasped, her grey gaze once again wide with apprehension. The damp of the fog seemed to have seeped into her very bones and she gave a slight shiver.

Good heavens, perhaps she really had stumbled on Dracula's castle, after all? Although she'd thought vampires only came out at night. Well, the heaviness of the damp fog hardly made it daylight, did it? She had been driving with her headlights on for the last two hours!

'Who—er, I mean, what—?' Crys began to take small steps backwards even as she formulated the question, positive that if she attempted to run the dog would have her down on the ground in seconds. The hound was obviously completely obedient to his master. A master who seemed more menacing by the second...

Not that he had looked particularly inviting in the first place. How to make a dignified exit? That was the problem.

Forget dignified—she just wanted out of here!

'You're right, Mr—er—I have taken up enough of your time.' She tried to smile as she spoke, but her cheeks refused to comply with the instruction, her lips twisting into a grimace rather than a smile. 'I'll just be on my way—'

'Where?'

She blinked at the abruptness of his question. 'I'm sorry...?'

The man scowled darkly. 'Not too many people come down this lane, let alone down the driveway; I asked where you were going,' he snapped.

Were going...!

This was obviously the cue for Crys to ask for directions to Sam Barton's house and be on her way. But now that it had come to the crunch she found she didn't want to tell this man exactly where she was going. Or why. But she had to say something!

She shrugged, shivering again as the damp fog penetrated her woollen jacket. 'I'm on my way to stay with friends.'

That was it; make sure that he knew she was expected somewhere, that someone would notice and call the police when she didn't arrive at her destination. Not that she was altogether sure Molly would go to that extreme; her friend would probably just assume Crys had changed her mind about coming to Yorkshire, after all. But this man didn't have to know that!

'I must have just taken a wrong turning in the fog,' she tried to dismiss lightly. 'I won't trouble you any further—'

'As I've already pointed out, Merlin is more troubled by your presence than I am,' the man drawled.

'He seems—calm enough now,' Crys attempted pleasantly. She remembered reading somewhere—she had no idea where!—that it was harder for someone to harm you if you established some sort of rapport with them, that an attacker was caught off-guard if the victim—

She was not a victim, damn it! She was merely a lost traveller who had stumbled upon—well, she wasn't sure what she had stumbled upon. But it was unnerving enough for her to know she wanted to leave. Now.

'Looks can be deceptive,' the man told her. 'Irish Wolfhounds, as a breed, are born hunters,' he continued almost conversationally. 'Instinctively trained to—'

'Are you deliberately trying to frighten me?' From somewhere—probably that same article that had advised building up a rapport!—she recalled that it was always better to attack rather than let oneself be attacked.

The man's mouth twisted into the semblance of a smile. 'Do I need to try?' he taunted.

Her cheeks coloured fiery-red at his obvious mockery. 'I'm not scared of you—'

'Aren't you?' He grimaced. 'Then you're giving a very good imitation of it!'

She gasped at the deliberate cruelty of his jibe. 'I am not—'

'There's a vein pulsing erratically at your left temple,' he cut in. 'Your pupils are dilated, the muscles in your face refuse to obey your commands, your body is tensed to rigidity, your hands are clenched so tightly into fists that you've probably made puncture marks in your palms with those nicely painted nails—' his gaze returned to her face '—and, unless I'm mistaken, despite the fact that you're obviously shivering with the cold, there's a very unbecoming bead of perspiration on your top lip.'

Everything he had said was true, Crys knew. But the fact that he was so aware of them too only served to make her angry at his unnecessary taunting.

'Women don't perspire—they glow!' she bit back, two bright wings of colour in her cheeks now, annoyed that, despite all her efforts, he seemed to have so easily gauged her emotions. 'This place is like something out of a Gothic horror story, guarded by the Hound of the Baskervilles. You step out of a grave to greet me, looking every inch as wild and savage as your—your hound—' she amended her words in an effort to stop the dog from growling once again '—and you expect me to look calm and collected!' She was breathing hard in her agitation, her fists clenched in frustrated anger now.

The man shrugged, apparently completely unperturbed by her outburst. 'I don't expect you to be anything,' he replied scathingly. 'I didn't invite you here.

I have no idea who you are. Nor do I have any interest in knowing,' he finished insultingly.

'And you have a grave to finish digging!' Crys inserted disgustedly.

'For a relation of Merlin's,' he explained. 'An Alsatian. We found him in the woods this morning.' He nodded tersely in the direction of a tarpaulin that lay on the ground several feet away, unnoticed by Crys until that moment.

A tarpaulin that obviously covered the body of a dead dog…

She swallowed hard. 'Doesn't he, or she, have an owner? Someone who—who needs to know about—? They might want to bury their pet themselves.' She couldn't take her gaze off the tarpaulin, her knees shaking in reaction, that shaking moving up the whole of her body as she spoke, even her voice beginning to quiver over the last few words.

'It probably did have an owner at one stage, but to my knowledge it's been living wild in the woods the last few months. The local farmers have been trying to capture it for weeks, because its been bothering sheep that are in lamb.' His mouth thinned. 'I guess one of them must have caught up with it.'

Crys's startled eyes searched the hardness of that partly obscured face. 'You mean—is that legal?' she choked as the full realisation of the dog's death began to hit her.

'Probably not. But proving it would be a problem,' he replied grimly.

Crys knew she had gone very pale—could feel the blood draining from her cheeks even as her fascinated gaze returned to the tarpaulin. 'I—do you think it was—quick?'

The man frowned his irritation. 'How should I know? Although, I doubt it. Poison is usually slow and insidious.'

'Poison?' Crys echoed faintly, eyes now huge in the paleness of her face, the band of freckles across the bridge of her nose standing out in stark relief.

He nodded abruptly. 'There are no wounds, no sign of any injury, in fact; poison is as good a guess as any for the cause of death.'

Death, death, and more death. Everywhere she looked—everywhere she went!—there was death!

It was Crys's last agonising thought before blackness engulfed her and she crumpled down onto the damp earth...

CHAPTER TWO

CRYS came back to consciousness feeling something rough against the side of her face and a rocking sensation which, since her head was already light and disorientated, threatened to bring on a bout of motion sickness.

She opened her eyes to find herself elevated off the ground, obviously being carried, her gaze widening with horror as she found herself looking up into the fiercely grim face of the man she now remembered owned an equally savage-looking dog. A dog that padded along at its master's side.

Crys opened her mouth—

'Don't you dare scream!' the man muttered between clenched teeth.

Crys closed her mouth as abruptly as she had opened it, totally startled by the fact that, even though he wasn't looking at her but grimly ahead, the man had realised she was once again fully conscious.

'If you scream I'm simply going to drop you where I stand,' the man added almost pleasantly.

As long as he—and his dog!—kept on walking, maybe that wouldn't be such a bad thing! It might at least give Crys a chance to run back to her car and get away from here.

'I've had one hell of a day already,' the man continued harshly. 'Finding that dog this morning was far from a pleasant way to start the day—quiet, Merlin!'

he bit out sharply as the dog began to growl at the unacceptable term. Merlin was instantly silenced.

Which only confirmed for Crys that of the two, and despite the animal's obvious size—and fierceness!—the man was the one to fear the most.

'I found the dead—canine this morning,' the man corrected, in deference to Merlin's sensitive feelings. 'I was trying to at least give it a decent burial by digging a grave in ground that hasn't thawed since November.' He flexed tired shoulder muscles. 'And then, finally to make my day, my privacy is invaded by a female with an overactive imagination who seems to consider that my only companion resembles a hound from hell—and that I'm right down there with him!' He viciously kicked a door open before striding forcefully into the house and into its kitchen. 'With hindsight, I should have just left you where you fell!' He dumped Crys down unceremoniously onto a chair before straightening and striding impatiently from the room.

Thankfully, the dog followed him!

Crys blinked dazedly, glad of the respite—no matter how brief!—from the man's overbearing personality. And his dog.

As her head finally began to clear it took her all of two seconds to realise that here was her chance to escape. Perhaps her only chance. She doubted—

She couldn't believe this kitchen!

The man had dumped her so ungraciously in a kitchen Crys could never have imagined in her wildest dreams. Never have imagined in this outwardly derelict castle, that was…

It was a beautiful room, with gorgeous mellow oak cupboards and a dark green Aga throwing out the heat that made the room deliciously warm after the cold January weather outside. A large oak work-table stood in the middle of the kitchen, and every implement a cook might need to work with hung from a rack overhead, with saucepans that gleamed with copper brightness. There was a stone-flagged floor beneath Crys's feet, in warm browns and creams, and the chair she sat on was one of the kitchen dining set of mellow oak.

After the lack of care and the decay on the outside, this kitchen was—incredible.

'Not what you were expecting, is it?'

Because of her utter surprise at these unexpected surroundings she had just lost her opportunity for escape, Crys realised.

She turned frowningly to look at her reluctant host. He stood silhouetted in the doorway, watching her from beneath hooded lids.

She took in his changed appearance—the overlong dark hair brushed into some semblance of order, the heavy black sweater removed in favour of a jumper of soft dark green cashmere. If the interior of the house was a surprise, then this man's changed appearance was equally so. But, to Crys's eyes, that didn't make him any more approachable.

Her expression showed her puzzlement. 'Why do you deliberately give the impression on the outside that the house is unlived-in?' She was pretty sure it *was* deliberate...

He raised dark brows, moving forward to place a copper kettle on top of the Aga before turning back to face her. 'Why do you think?' he drawled scathingly.

He looked younger now he wasn't looming out of

the fog, and, without the bulky jumper, taller and
leaner too. The face beneath the growth of beard appeared unlined. Crys put his age somewhere in his
thirties. In fact, now that she could see him more
clearly, there was something vaguely familiar about
him...

Although no amount of feelings of familiarity
could dispel the hard mockery in that dark green
gaze!

Crys grimaced. 'To keep at bay females with overactive imaginations...?'

Very white teeth showed briefly in the semblance
of a grin. 'In one,' he confirmed with satisfaction,
turning to remove the boiling kettle from the Aga.
'Tea or coffee?'

After her terrifying thoughts of a few minutes
ago—evoked by such an overactive imagination?—
this man's polite offer of a hot drink seemed slightly
ludicrous. Or maybe she was the one who was ludicrous...?

'Coffee. Thanks,' she accepted distractedly as he
took a tin and cups out of one of the cupboards, his
back towards her. She reached up to remove her hat
and unwind the scarf at her throat, now she was
warmed by the heat of the room. 'Er—where's
Merlin?' she added somewhat nervously; the hound
hadn't returned with his master.

'Off chasing rabbits, I expect,' his owner dismissed
unconcernedly. 'I let him out of the front door a few
minutes—' he broke off abruptly.

Crys was so distracted by the comfort of her surroundings, the welcome warmth after hours of driving
through cold damp fog, that for a few seconds she
didn't even realise he had stopped talking. She sat

back in her chair, her eyes closed, as she began to thaw out. But she slowly became aware of a charged silence, the very air about her seeming to crackle with electricity.

She turned back to her host, colour warming her cheeks as she saw the way he stared gloweringly across the room at her. She knew what he would see, of course; long silver-blonde hair cascading silkily down her back, its colour even more startling against the black of her coat, eyes of clear grey, a light dusting of freckles over the bridge of her uptilted nose, her mouth wide and pouting, even if unsmiling at the moment.

Perhaps she had been a little precipitate in relaxing her guard enough to remove her scarf and hat…

She waited for his startled expression to change to one of recognition, steeling herself for what he would say next, her tension rising as he said nothing.

She swallowed hard, pointed chin raised challengingly. 'Not what you were expecting either?' She deliberately put a taunting lilt in her voice. Perhaps he hadn't recognised her after all…?

Green eyes narrowed icily. 'I wasn't expecting *you* at all!' he responded.

He really hadn't recognised her!

But even if *he* wasn't expecting her, someone else was, and the sooner she made her excuses and went on her way the better she would like it.

She stood up. 'Perhaps I won't bother with the coffee, after all—'

'It's made now.' He put the mug of coffee down heavily on the table in front of her, consequently standing much closer to her than was comfortable.

'You look cold. Drink it,' he urged as she would have protested.

Crys wasn't at all happy with his dictatorial tone. But in the circumstances, still uncertain of the man—and his mood!—she was hardly in a position to object.

He sat down opposite her at the table, looking at her expectantly as he cradled his own mug of warming coffee in large, well-kept hands.

Crys slowly sat down again, the smell of the rich coffee tantalising to her senses, she had to inwardly admit. It had been some time since her last rest stop; the coffee at the service station had been tepid and weak to say the least. Perhaps it wouldn't do any harm to drink this mug of coffee before going on her way.

Besides, the unfriendly Merlin was outside somewhere, making it impossible for her to leave without this man's protection. She frowned as another thought occurred to her. Perhaps that was the reason this man had put Merlin back outside...

'An overactive imagination *and* a suspicious mind,' the man pronounced, without even glancing across at her. 'What a combination!' He gave a disgusted shake of his head before sipping his black unsweetened coffee. 'What comes next, I wonder...?' he mused, glancing over at her, one dark brow raised sceptically. 'Drugs in your drink? So that you don't put up a fight when I carry you upstairs with the intention of having my wicked way with you?'

Crys's cheeks coloured fiery-red at the laughter that could clearly be heard in his voice, but at the same time she glanced worriedly at the mug in front of her.

'Tell me,' the man continued in that deceptively pleasant voice, 'do you watch a lot of television?'

His implication was more than obvious! But, as she had already pointed out to him, the last half an hour or so had been far from pleasant for her, either. She was the one who had found herself face to face with that growling monster of a dog and had then been confronted by a wild-looking man digging a grave— who had given every appearance of being more fierce than his dog.

Overactive imagination, indeed!

She gave him a humourless smile. 'As it happens, I don't even own a television!'

He grimaced. 'Then perhaps you should.'

She didn't seem able to win where this man was concerned! 'I read a lot. Agatha Christie, mostly.' She answered the question defensively before he could even ask it.

He relaxed back in his chair, watching her with dark, unfathomable eyes. 'Then this must seem like the perfect setting for a murder to you,' he accepted. 'A derelict, apparently empty castle. Guarded by a fierce hound. Inhabited by a darkly unwelcoming man.'

On the surface, all of that was true, and it was what she had initially thought. But in this warmly comfortable setting, with a steaming mug of coffee in front of her, this man no longer seemed quite so formidable. She'd already deduced by his voice that he was a well-educated man, and the removal of that bulky black jumper had revealed that he wore clothes Crys was pretty sure carried exclusive labels.

As for the dog… Well, for the moment he was safely outside.

And the castle itself... Crys was sure this man's earlier answer, concerning the obvious dereliction outside, so in contrast to its comfortable interior, had been deliberately over-simplified—had merely been an avoidance of the true answer.

This man, she was sure, was playing with her. But not in the way of an attacker with his proposed victim, more as a way of self-defence. Which begged the question—what did he have to hide?

She drew in a sharp breath. 'Mr—I don't believe I caught your name...?' She raised blonde brows questioningly.

He met her gaze unblinkingly. 'I don't believe I gave it,' he replied hardly.

She was well aware of that, damn him. But she had thought that good manners would— Good manners! What was she thinking of? This man had no reason to be in the least polite to her, let alone introduce himself.

A fact he was all too well aware of, if the knowing smile that now curved his lips was anything to go by!

'Or that you told me yours,' he added pointedly.

He was right, Crys decided stubbornly, there was absolutely no need for the two of them to be in the least polite to each other. Besides, she felt a reluctance to tell this man anything more about herself than he already knew.

She stood up, wrapping her scarf back about her throat. 'It's getting late.' She looked pointedly out of the window at the increasing darkness through the foggy haze. 'I have somewhere else to go.'

Her chances of finding Sam Barton's home before it became too dark to see anything were pretty slim now, she realised, but she would probably be able to find a hotel somewhere, and could give Molly a ring from there.

'If you wouldn't mind seeing me safely to my car,' she prompted, as the man made no effort to stand up. 'Merlin may not take too kindly to my going outside alone.' In fact she was sure, without this man's presence, that she wouldn't get any further than the door before Merlin showed his displeasure!

'Probably not,' her reluctant host acknowledged dryly.

Crys held her breath as she waited for his next move. If he stood up to see her safely to her car, then all the misgivings she had had where he was concerned *were* simply her overactive imagination, but if he made no move—

She gave a nervous start as the telephone on the wall began to ring shrilly in the silence of the kitchen, her hat falling to the floor in her agitation.

'It's only the telephone,' the man drawled derisively as he stood up, green eyes glittering with laughter now.

At her expense, Crys knew. But driving in the fog for several hours had already strung her nerves out to breaking point. This unexpected encounter with this man and his gigantic dog had done nothing at all to ease her tension!

'I know what it is,' she snapped, before bending impatiently to pick up her hat, her face slightly red from the exertion as she straightened to find him still watching her. 'Aren't you going to answer it?' She frowned as he continued to let the telephone ring. 'It could be important.'

He shrugged unconcernedly. 'It could be.'

The monotonous ring of the telephone began to

grate on her already frazzled nerves. 'Well?' she said sharply.

He tilted his head, listening, finally giving a terse nod of his head as the telephone was abruptly silenced.

'There now,' Crys said with satisfaction.

'Twelve rings before ringing off.' He nodded.

'Twelve...? But—' She broke off as the telephone began to ring again.

'Twelve rings, ring off, then ring again, and it's family,' the man told her moving to pick up the receiver.

Crys frowned at this explanation. She couldn't have said how many times the telephone had rung before it had stopped, hadn't been aware that this man was counting them, either.

'And if it's not twelve rings before ringing off?' she found herself asking dazedly.

He put one large hand over the mouthpiece of the telephone, his expression grim. 'Then it doesn't get answered,' he replied economically.

What a strange, strange man, Crys decided with a barely perceptible shake of her head. He lived in this crumbling castle in what appeared to be complete solitude, except for a dog half the size of a horse, chose to answer his telephone only when he was sure the call was from a member of his family, obviously finding any other contact from outside his solitary world a complete intrusion—and yet at the same time he felt enough compassion at the death of a wild dog to dig it a grave in ground that had been frozen for weeks.

Enigmatic hardly began to describe such behavior. He was completely beyond Crys's comprehension—

'Is it okay if I answer this now?' He held up the receiver with his hand over the mouthpiece. 'Or do you have any other questions that need answering before I do?' He quirked mocking brows.

Once again Crys felt that flush in her cheeks. 'Go ahead,' she invited dryly, turning away from the mockery in his gaze to move listlessly about the kitchen.

She would have liked to be able to leave altogether while he took the call, but she was still too all aware of the slavering Merlin patrolling outside. Besides—

Crys came to an abrupt halt in her aimless meandering, suddenly arrested by something this man had said on the one side of the conversation she could hear.

'Just cut out the excuses, Molly, and tell me exactly when you do expect to get here?' he barked impatiently. 'The day after tomorrow?' He obviously repeated the answer he received. 'And exactly what am I expected to do with your guest until you do decide to put in an appearance?' he added exasperatedly.

Crys was staring at him now, eyes wide with disbelief. *Molly.* He had named his caller as Molly!

'Very funny,' he retorted scathingly at the reply he received, shooting Crys an irritated look as he realised she was openly listening to the conversation. 'Look, Molly, this was not part of the deal. I agreed to letting you bring this Chris here for a few days on condition you kept the parents off my back over Christmas— yes, I know you did that by inviting them to New York to stay with you. But that doesn't alter the fact that you can't just expect to dump this man on me while you— What did you just say?' He became suddenly still, appearing all the more menacing because of that stillness.

Crys gave a wince, well able to imagine what Molly had only just informed him.

He had named his caller as Molly. And she lived in New York… It was too much of a coincidence for Crys to be wrong in the conclusion she had come to.

This man—unbelievable as it might seem!—had to be Sam Barton. Molly's brother. And until a few seconds ago Sam had thought Molly was bringing a man called Chris to stay with him for a few days. She was sure he was no longer under *that* particular misapprehension!

She sensed Sam's emerald gaze on her now, as an unpalatable thought obviously occurred to him, so she deliberately kept her own eyes averted from what she knew would now be his hard, accusing ones.

This was awful! Worse than anything she could ever have imagined!

This man was the older brother Molly so adored!

Crys had agreed, very reluctantly, after Molly's constant badgering of her, to spend a few days with her at the Yorkshire home of her older brother. But Molly was warm and bubbly, extremely caring—was probably the best friend Crys had ever had—whereas this man—Molly's brother, Sam!—on their short acquaintance, appeared to have none of those attributes!

'No, Molly.' Sam was talking dryly to his sister now. 'I will not frighten your friend away by doing my Heathcliff impression. Yes, I'll tell her how sorry you are not to be here when she arrives. Yes, I'll make her welcome.' Impatience entered his voice now. '"Be kind to her"…?' he repeated slowly, green gaze openly taunting at the colour that had entered

Crys's heated cheeks. 'What do you think, Molly?'
he derided.

Crys inwardly panicked. It wasn't a question of
what her friend thought; she already knew for herself
that kindness was not necessarily a natural part of this
man's nature.

'I'll do my best.' Sam suddenly chuckled, a pleasantly husky sound.

Although not particularly so to Crys. This man had
terrified the life out of her the first time she saw him,
had been alternately caustic and mocking since that
time; there was no way she could agree to stay here
alone with him for a couple of days while she waited
for Molly's belated arrival!

She stepped forward. 'Could I—?'

'Yes, Molly, I will remember to tell Chris how
sorry you are. Talk to you later,' Sam firmly finished,
before replacing the receiver, his gaze challenging as
he turned back to Crys.

Crys stared back at him with widely apprehensive
eyes. Knowing he was Molly's brother, after all, had
done nothing to alleviate her apprehension…!

CHAPTER THREE

CRYS mentally shook herself. 'That was Molly on the telephone, wasn't it?' she said heavily.

His mouth twisted derisively. 'Very astute of you—considering I called her by her name several times!'

Crys decided to ignore Sam Barton's obvious sarcasm—it simply wouldn't help the situation if she lost her temper with him. Although…she wasn't sure anything could improve the immediate situation!

'And you're her brother, Sam,' she said evenly.

Although two people more unalike Crys couldn't imagine! Molly was small and red-haired, with warm brown eyes, a gamine and beautiful face, and one of the friendliest natures Crys had ever known. Sam Barton was none of those things!

'A regular Einstein, in fact,' he drawled.

Despite her earlier resolve, Crys felt her anger towards this man rising, her cheeks hot with the emotion. This situation was already bad enough, without his unwarranted sarcasm!

'Mr Barton—'

'Sam will do,' he cut in. 'I take it you're Chris? Short for?' he prompted at her nod of confirmation.

'Crystal,' she supplied reluctantly, considering the question quite inappropriate in the circumstances.

That hard green gaze raked over her mercilessly, from her tiny feet, her obvious slenderness, to the tip of her silver-blonde head.

'It figures,' he finally drawled insultingly.

'Why does it?' she came back sharply.

He shrugged broad shoulders. 'You look as if the slightest thing might snap you in half.'

'Looks can be deceptive,' she returned, with pointed reference to his remark earlier concerning Merlin's docility.

'Touché.' His mouth twisted into a humourless smile, that hard gaze once again raking over her with complete disregard for the fact that he was being extremely rude.

Crys was well aware of the fact that she had lost a considerable amount of weight due to the strain of the last year. Her small frame, along with her diminutive height—only a little over five feet—gave her an air of fragility that might otherwise not have been there. Her face was thin, cheekbones prominent beneath haunted grey eyes, jawline finely visible. Only the fullness of her mouth remained the same.

She had hoped that this few days in Yorkshire with Molly might help to alleviate some of that strain— but only a few minutes' acquaintance with Molly's older brother had shown Crys that wasn't going to happen!

'Well, Crys, it looks as if you don't have somewhere else to go, after all,' Sam taunted.

That was what he thought! 'I take it, from what was said, that Molly isn't going to be here for a couple more days?'

Even that humourless smile disappeared now. 'You take it correctly,' he confirmed grimly. 'The rehearsals for the film she starts shooting next month have run over schedule,' he explained briefly, before picking up his empty mug and moving to pour a refill. 'Want one?' he offered belatedly.

'No, thank you,' she returned primly, aware that his lack of manners in not offering her more coffee before was probably due to the fact that he spent most of his time here alone—that he wasn't used to catering to the needs of a guest. It wasn't a feeling she, personally, intended altering for him, either! She was also aware that, as an actress, Molly had a schedule often disturbed in this way. It was one of the reasons they had decided to drive up separately to Yorkshire. 'As Molly can't make it for a while, I think it would be better—' for all of them! '—if I—'

'I hope you aren't going to suggest booking into a hotel,' Sam rasped, shaking his head. 'Molly would never forgive me if I allowed you to do that.'

Now it was Crys's turn to give a humourless smile. 'And I'm sure that would bother you!'

'As a matter of fact—yes, it would,' he replied firmly. 'Molly is very dear to me.' His voice was husky now. 'She's—special. And any friend of hers is welcome here,' he added with finality.

Crys silently agreed with him about Molly being special. The two girls had met at boarding-school ten years ago, when Molly had joined the lower sixth in preparation for taking her 'A' Levels. For anyone else, a change of school at such a delicate time might have resulted in feeling lost and out of place, but Molly's nature was such that she quickly made herself at home wherever she was. The two girls had quickly become fast friends, spending most of their time together during school term.

Curiously enough, though, they had never visited each other at home during the holidays... If they had, Crys would already have known that she felt most uncomfortable in the presence of Molly's brother who was twelve years older!

'Unless I'm mistaken, you were under the impression that Molly's friend Crys was a man?' she asked.

'Molly was most insistent that I be nice to this particular friend. It was important to her that this Chris should feel welcome. It was a natural assumption to have made, in the circumstances.'

Crys felt a glow of warmth at her friend's obvious care for her comfort. Although that didn't change the fact that Sam Barton had now been presented with a female friend rather than the male he had been expecting, or that Molly's arrival had been delayed for a couple of days...

'That was kind of Molly,' she accepted. 'Although her unexpected absence does change things rather—'

'Because you're a woman and not the man I was expecting?' He frowned darkly. 'Why does that change anything?'

Surely that was more than obvious, even to a man who chose to live as out of touch with the world as this one did? Oh, not that Crys felt in the least prudish about the fact that they would be a man and woman staying alone here for a few days. Despite her earlier imaginings, this man hadn't given the least indication that he found her in the least attractive, let alone anything else. It was just that he was so obviously somebody who preferred his own company—possibly with the exception of Molly's—that having a complete stranger foisted on him for a couple of days simply wasn't on.

Besides, though Molly had always talked about her older brother in glowing terms, there was something decidedly odd about a thirty-eight-year-old man living reclusively in the wilds of Yorkshire in a castle that was deliberately made to look derelict on the outside but was the height of luxury inside!

Added to which, Crys didn't feel in the least comfortable with him—would find it absolute purgatory to have to spend days alone here with him.

'It really is very kind of you to make such an offer, Mr Barton—'

'The name is Sam,' he rasped. 'And I'm sure, even on such brief acquaintance—' his mouth twisted derisively '—that you are well aware that kindness is not a predominant part of my nature!'

Oh, yes, she was aware, all right, had believed him earlier when he'd threatened to drop her if she screamed.

She shook her head. 'Nevertheless—'

'Look, as you pointed out earlier, it's getting late, and the light's fading fast,' he cut in briskly. 'I need to go outside for a while and—and finish what I started. Why don't you make yourself at home here for an hour or so and we'll talk about this again when I come back?'

Yes, he *would* have dropped her earlier, Crys had no doubt, but she reminded herself that he also had enough compassion in him to give a decent burial to a stray dog he had found dead this morning...

'Pour yourself another coffee,' he invited lightly, 'warm yourself next to the Aga. And we'll see how you feel about things later. Okay?'

The cup of coffee and the Aga sounded inviting, but Crys was already sure how she would feel about things later; she simply couldn't stay here with this man. He might be Molly's brother, and Molly obviously adored him, but Crys wasn't sure she even liked him!

She looked up to find his green gaze still regarding her searchingly, although the blandness of his expression gave away none of what he was thinking.

Crys looked at him now with the knowledge that he was Molly's beloved brother, desperately trying to see the man her friend talked about with such love and pride. He was a writer, she knew that much about him, although she had no idea what sort of books he wrote. It did perhaps explain why he chose to live in this remote place—but not the reason for the deliberately deceptive dereliction outside!

No, there was something not quite right about this situation—and with all the other upsets she had had in her life this last year she did not want to become a part of it.

'Molly is going to be very disappointed if she rings back and I tell her you've chosen to stay at a hotel until she arrives,' he said suddenly.

Were her thoughts so transparent? Crys wondered with dismay—because that was exactly what she had been about to tell him!

But he was right about Molly's disappointment. Her friend simply wouldn't understand if she went to a hotel instead of waiting for her here.

Crys shook her head. 'You can't really want me to stay here.' She grimaced, sure that company—her company especially!—was the last thing this man wanted. After all, he had made his opinion of her only too obvious earlier.

'No,' he confirmed bluntly. 'But for Molly's sake I'm willing to put up with it.'

And, his unspoken words implied, so should you be!

He was right, of course. Molly was one of the most kind-hearted people on earth—had invited Crys here because she wanted to help her come to terms with the last year. To choose not to stay here after all, simply because Molly had been delayed a few days, was ungrateful in the extreme. Not that Molly would ever say so, but she would be hurt, nonetheless.

'As I said, think about it,' Sam advised harshly, before striding forcefully from the room. The front door slammed a few seconds later as he left the house, instantly greeted by the sound of Merlin's joyful barking.

Crys's breath left her in a sigh as soon as Sam was out of the room. She sank down gratefully onto one of the kitchen chairs as she tried to collect her thoughts.

Think about Molly, Sam had meant by that last remark. He was right, of course. But, even so, Crys was loath to agree to stay here with Sam while she waited for Molly to arrive. What would the two of them talk about, for one thing? He certainly didn't appear to be a man blessed with any of the social graces, so small talk was probably out!

What a mess!

Her first social venture out in a very long time, and she found herself cosily ensconced with the most unwelcoming man she had ever met in her life, miles from civilisation—or at least so it seemed—with the fog seeming to cocoon them in eerie solitude.

The fog!

A brief glance out of the kitchen window showed Crys that, instead of lifting, as she had hoped it might, the fog had in fact thickened. So much so that she could see absolutely nothing now except that silvery blanket.

Great. Even the weather seemed to be conspiring against her!

She was going to look more than a little churlish if she insisted on leaving in weather like this—she was going to look as if she were running away. From Sam Barton!

But wasn't she? Didn't the man unnerve her to the point of giving her the jitters? He—

She looked up as the front door opened and then once more closed with a resounding slam, her gaze apprehensive as Merlin preceded his master into the kitchen. The dog really was as enormous as he had appeared outside, filling half the doorway as he came to an abrupt halt, hackles once again rising at her presence there, looking at her with pale canine eyes.

'She's a friend, Merlin,' Sam told the dog impatiently as he shifted the animal out of the way so that he could come into the kitchen as well, bringing a draught of cold air with him as he moved to warm his hands on the Aga. 'I'm afraid that particular job is going to have to wait until the morning, when hopefully I'll be able to see what I'm doing.'

'The fog is worse, isn't it?' Crys said unnecessarily, hoping this gigantic dog understood the meaning of the word 'friend'—although, in all truth, she hardly came into that category!

Sam's grin was as wolfish as his dog's growl had been earlier. 'I wouldn't even send Merlin out on a night like this!'

His meaning wasn't lost on Crys and she shot him an impatient look. 'In that case, I accept your kind offer of hospitality. For tonight, at least,' she added quickly when Sam gave a grimace of satisfaction at her capitulation.

He nodded abruptly as he straightened. 'At least you've chosen not to add foolhardy to your other more obvious…character traits,' he drawled mockingly.

Faults, he meant, Crys easily realised. Maybe he should take a look at himself some time!

She drew in a sharp breath. 'Perhaps if you could tell me where I'm to sleep? Then I can go and get my case from the car and indulge myself with a hot bath.' Her shoulders and neck ached from the hours of driving, and with her recent loss of weight the cold seemed to have penetrated to her bones. 'If that's convenient, of course,' she added belatedly; after all, just because this room was cosily warm and modern did not mean that upstairs there was the luxury of a bathroom and hot running water.

'Of course,' Sam echoed dryly. 'I forgot to ask earlier—can you cook?'

Crys frowned. 'I beg your pardon?'

'I'm sure it hasn't escaped your notice that I live alone here? I manage for myself the majority of the time—stews, things like that—but it can get slightly monotonous; Molly usually cooks for me when she comes to stay.' He quirked expectant brows in Crys's direction.

In other words, she was going to have to cook for her supper—and his, apparently!

'Yes, Mr—Sam,' she amended as he grimaced, 'I can cook,' she assured him dryly. 'Did you have anything particular in mind?' she added ruefully.

'Molly's speciality is stuffed rainbow trout for

starters, followed by roast fillet of beef with all the trimmings,' he came back instantly.

'I see.' Crys held back her smile with effort—after all, she really had little to smile about! 'Do I take it you have the ingredients for that particular meal?' Of course he did—he would hardly have mentioned it otherwise!

'In the fridge,' he confirmed unnecessarily.

As she had thought. Oh, well, perhaps cooking dinner was the least she could do in return for the comfort of having a roof over her head when the elements were so unwelcoming outside.

Except the elements inside—namely Molly's brother Sam!—weren't too welcoming either!

But cooking dinner might infuse some sort of normality into this otherwise strange situation.

'If you've finished your coffee, I'll take you upstairs.' Sam threw his coat over one of the kitchen chairs before turning decisively towards the door.

In other words, she *had* finished her coffee. At least, as far as Sam was concerned.

She picked up her hat and scarf before following him out of the room, curious now to see the rest of the interior, sure that it was going to be—

Crys came to a halt in the spacious hallway; a huge oak table stood in its centre and the most magnificent oak staircase led to the wide gallery above. But it was the dome in the ceiling above them, and the long crystal chandelier that was suspended from it, that held her spellbound. Not just the gold filigree work in the dome itself, but also the telling artwork on one of the panels.

'James…' she breathed dazedly, unable to tear her gaze away from that telltale trademark.

'What did you say?' Sam asked impatiently, having come to a halt partway up the wide staircase as he realised she was no longer following him.

Crys blinked, frowning as she turned towards the sound of his voice, taking several seconds to return to reality.

She moistened dry lips. 'I was—I—James Webber was your interior designer,' she finally managed to murmur.

James had been here. Had worked in this house. He'd probably stood exactly where she was standing now as he'd critically appraised his own work.

Sam gave an acknowledging inclination of his head. 'He was,' he confirmed. 'But how did you know that?' he demanded.

For the second time today Crys was feeling slightly faint, knew also that her face had paled dramatically. But she didn't dare pass out again in this man's company; he would wonder what on earth he had been landed with if she did!

It was just the shock of seeing James's work so suddenly—of knowing that he had been here, that perhaps he'd stood on this very spot...

'When did he do this?' She couldn't stop herself asking. James had never mentioned visiting Molly's brother in a castle in Yorkshire to her.

'About three years ago now.' Sam walked back down the six stairs he had already ascended, his gaze narrowed to green slits as he eyed her warily. 'I asked how you knew it was Webber's work?' he demanded again as he came to stand in front of her.

Crys gave a poignant smile as she looked around her. 'It's very distinctive, don't you think?' she murmured wistfully. The hallway was decorated in a mixture of warm reds and golds, the carpet up the stairs was a glorious scarlet, and then there was that telltale dome, with its yellow artwork.

'Very,' Sam snapped. 'But that doesn't answer my question.'

Her gaze returned reluctantly to the grimness of Sam's face, and she was jolted by the hard look of suspicion she could easily see there. 'Don't look so worried, Mr—Sam,' she said softly. 'You see the tiny yellow rose up in the dome? On the left side panel?' She pointed it out as Sam looked up. 'James always sneaked a yellow rose in somewhere. It was his trademark.'

'Was?' Sam echoed sharply.

'He died,' Crys said abruptly, swallowing hard, forcing herself to remain calm. After all, she was only stating what was an indisputable fact. 'A year ago. He had cancer.'

A disease as insidious as the poison Sam had mentioned earlier. A disease that struck indiscriminately, both at the young and the old, the talented, the weak and the strong.

'I didn't know...' Sam replied slowly. 'Molly introduced him to me. He was a friend of hers from university days.' He shook his head. 'She didn't mention that he had died.'

No, Molly probably wouldn't have talked of James's death. She had been almost as shocked as Crys when it had happened. And the two of them had never talked of it since, either...

'I suppose that's how you knew him too,' Sam murmured thoughtfully. 'Molly must have introduced the two of you,' he elaborated at Crys's puzzled expression.

Yes, Molly had introduced Crys and James to each other, eighteen months ago. An introduction that had been love at first sight for both of them.

But there was something Crys wasn't revealing to Sam about James. Something that was still so painful there was no way she could tell this strange, reclusive man about it.

James Webber had been her husband...

CHAPTER FOUR

'DO YOU have everything you need?'

Crys turned from placing the beef joint in the Aga, her eyes wide as she slowly straightened to look across the kitchen at Sam as he stood in the doorway. If she had thought his change of clothes earlier had made a vast difference to his disreputable appearance, then the shaving off of several days' growth of beard had brought about a complete transformation. Underneath all that he was actually a very attractive man, she realised with an unpleasant jolt.

His face was tanned—probably from hours spent outside during the summer months—his eyes deeply green against the darkness of his skin. His nose was long and straight, he had a chiselled mouth, a lower lip that was sensuously full and his jaw was square and firm. The darkness of his hair showed it was still damp from the shower he had obviously just taken. The dark green shirt and black tailored trousers he wore were also an improvement on what he had been sporting earlier.

Crys was once again assailed with a feeling of familiarity—which was ridiculous; if she had ever met this man before she would have remembered it!

As if aware of at least part of the reason for her surprise, he ran a hand ruefully over the smoothness of his shaven chin. 'I get a little lazy being here on my own so much,' he acknowledged dryly. 'Molly would have insisted I smarten myself up when she arrived,' he added derisively.

Crys gave a smile. 'That's what younger sisters are for, I believe.'

Sam strode confidently into the kitchen. 'Do you have any brothers or sisters?' he asked interestedly.

Her smile instantly faded. 'No,' she answered quietly. 'And, to answer your earlier question, yes, I have everything here that I need to make the meal.'

The bedroom Sam had shown her into a little over an hour ago, with its turquoise and cream décor, had proved as pleasing as the rest of the interior of the house. Although, given the misapprehension Sam had been under concerning the gender of the guest Molly was bringing with her, Crys had wisely not mentioned the fact that there was a double bed in the room!

The adjoining turquoise and cream bathroom had proved just as opulent once Sam had left her alone to unpack, and she had spent an hour in the sunken bath, just luxuriating in hot scented water.

That hour of unadulterated indulgence had gone a long way to settling her earlier agitation at having to stay here alone with Sam. Although she accepted that another reason for her feeling of calm was the fact she could now feel James's presence in the house, knew that he had been here, that he had been the one to decorate the interior so lovingly. Albeit under Sam's instructions.

'Anything I can do?' Sam offered now. 'I feel a little guilty now at asking you to cook the meal,' he admitted ruefully. 'Spending so much time alone, my manners aren't always what they should be, either,' he acknowledged.

Crys looked at him consideringly, realising that this was as close to an apology for his earlier behaviour as she was likely to get. She had no doubts that it was probably only being made at all because she was a friend of his sister's; despite his attempt to appear affable, Sam didn't give the impression that he particularly cared what anyone thought of his manners, good or otherwise!

'A glass of wine might be rather nice. White, to go with the trout, if that's okay?' She smiled, warm and comfortable in a pale blue jumper and blue denims that she'd changed into after her bath. 'Did Molly tell you anything about me?' she prompted as he moved to choose a bottle of wine from the wine cooler Crys had already found in one of the cupboards.

'Obviously not,' he replied as he opened the bottle. 'Otherwise I wouldn't have been expecting a man!'

'Hmm,' she murmured softly, accepting one of the two glasses of wine he had poured and sipping it appreciatively. He might be the most anti-social person she had ever met, but he certainly knew how to choose a good wine! 'We were at school together—'

'You're Cryssy!' he suddenly guessed, eyes wide. 'I remember now. She used to talk about you incessantly when she came home from school. It was 'Cryssy this' and 'Cryssy that',' he recalled, using the name the girls had given her at school.

'Oh, dear.' Crys grimaced. 'If it's any consolation, she used to talk about *you* incessantly during our time at school,' she returned teasingly.

'Indeed?' He became suddenly still, looking at her over the top of his wine glass. 'What did she used to say?' he asked casually.

Too casually, Crys realised frowningly, knowing

that Sam was eyeing her in his wary way once again. 'Nothing detrimental, I assure you,' she responded soothingly. What on earth did he think Molly, who so obviously adored him, would have said about him other than to praise him to the skies?

If she remembered correctly, Molly had implied that her older brother wasn't like other men—that, if asked, he could do the equivalent of walking on water. Well, Crys agreed with her friend about the first bit—Sam was like no other man she had ever met!

She decided it might be prudent right now to change the subject. 'I wasn't sure whether we would be eating in here or in the dining room?' She presumed one of the shuttered rooms downstairs *was* a dining room...

'Here. If that's okay with you?' Then he added as an afterthought, 'It will be warmer than the dining room.'

Crys managed to hold back her smile this time at his effort at good manners; after all, he was trying! 'Fine.' She nodded. 'In that case, perhaps you would like to lay the table? That way I can carry on with pan-frying the trout.'

Very domesticated, she thought wryly, as the two of them moved economically about the kitchen, carrying out their own individual tasks.

Too domesticated, Crys acknowledged frowningly several minutes later, as she realised she was actually humming softly to herself as she cooked the trout.

Despite the fact that it was the rude Sam Barton she was with, she hadn't felt this relaxed in a very long time. Too long, she decided with a nervous sideways glance in his direction. Sam was a puzzle, a reclusive mystery man. Not a man it was wise to relax with. And she hadn't been so long without male company that she should fall into the trap of relaxing her guard. Not even for a minute!

'I hope you enjoy it,' she said stiffly a few minutes later when she placed a plate of trout on the table in front of him before moving back to the Aga to deal with the vegetables for the main course.

'Aren't you having any?'

She turned to find him looking across the kitchen at her. Giving a rueful shake of her head, she said apologetically, 'I'll never eat the beef if I eat the trout first.' Her appetite just wasn't up to eating huge meals any more.

'Sit,' Sam instructed, and stood up to get another plate, crossing back to the table to cut the trout in half. 'I said, sit,' he rasped as she made no effort to do so.

'I am not Merlin, Mr Barton—'

'And I'm not Mr anything! I told you—my name is Sam,' he snapped coldly. 'And I'm fully aware you aren't Merlin—he does as he's told!'

Crys glared at him, grey gaze clashing with green. It was a war of wills—and, after several tension-filled seconds, Crys wasn't sure she was going to be able to keep it up much longer!

'Will it help if I say please?' Sam suddenly murmured huskily.

It would help a great deal. It would also give her a face-saving way of backing away from the tension that had suddenly sprung up between them again.

Except she really didn't want to sit down and eat trout with him. For one thing it would ruin her main meal. For another—she was suddenly finding this closeness in the cosiness of the kitchen *too* close!

What on earth was wrong with her? James had died a year ago, yes, but the year since then had been traumatic, to say the least—far too emotionally fraught for her to even think of another man in a romantic way. Besides, she wasn't a woman who needed a man in her life just to feel complete.

Then why was she suddenly so aware of Sam…?

'What is it?'

She looked up to find Sam watching her searchingly, looking quickly away again as her awareness of him intensified.

The man was rude, aggressive, totally without charm, she told herself firmly.

Yes, but he was also compassionate concerning animals. He'd apologised for that earlier rudeness. And he was trying his hardest now to be polite. Plus, Molly obviously adored him…!

'The trout's getting cold,' Sam said pointedly as she still didn't answer him.

Crys reluctantly took her place opposite his at the table, deep in thought as she picked up her knife and fork and began to eat, aware that the feeling of relaxed well-being of a short time ago had completely evaporated.

Maybe, if the fog lifted tomorrow, she could go out for a drive? It would give both her and Sam a respite from each other while they waited for Molly to arrive the following day.

Who was she kidding? It would give her a respite from a man whose company she was starting to find completely overpowering!

'You look like a little girl who's being made to eat up her greens,' Sam muttered with distaste.

Crys looked at him blankly for several seconds,

giving a smile as she finally took in what he had said. 'Have *you* tasted the trout yet?' she asked dryly, taking another sip of her wine.

'I haven't had a chance!' He sighed, forking up a mouthful, and a smile of complete appreciation immediately curved those sculptured lips, his eyes closing in ecstasy. 'I thought Molly's trout was pretty good, but if anything this is even better!' he responded a few minutes later.

Crys gave an impish grin. 'I promise not to tell her you said that! Although it's nice to know my recipe is appreciated,' she rejoined softly.

'*Your* recipe?' Sam's eyes opened wide.

She nodded. 'And my star pupil continues to cook it so capably,' she added teasingly, tasting some of her own fish now, her critical taste telling her that it could have taken a squeeze more lemon. But otherwise, yes, it was up to standard.

'Okay.' Sam grimaced in surrender. 'Explain, if you please.'

'I'm a professional chef,' she told him simply, which was why she had smiled to herself earlier when he had asked her if she could cook.

'And?' He ate some more of his trout as he waited for her answer.

'And nothing,' she replied. 'Molly and I worked together for a bit one time when she was 'resting'. She actually enjoyed herself—thought of changing professions for a while. But then the offer of a play came up and she was off to her first love again.' Crys gave an affectionate smile at the memory of those fun-filled weeks of working with Molly.

'But this trout is your own personal recipe...?' Sam

said slowly, watching her intently over the rim of his wine glass.

'I love cooking,' she dismissed lightly.

'Hmm.' Sam said thoughtfully. 'Why do I get the impression there's something you aren't telling me…?'

Crys laughed softly, shaking her head. 'I believe that works both ways, Sam!' In fact, this man had told her absolutely nothing about himself. 'For instance, I believe you're a writer?'

'Who told you I'm a writer?' he barked, suddenly tense again, the easy companionship of a few minutes ago completely disappearing as he looked at her with narrowed eyes. 'Don't tell me,' he bit out disgustedly. 'Molly!'

Crys frowned at this sudden change in him. 'I'm sorry, I didn't know it was supposed to be a secret. You probably write under a pseudonym, anyway, so I doubt—'

'And just what makes you think I would write under a pseudonym?' Sam cut in, his gaze glacial now.

The pleasantries definitely seemed to be over for the evening! But how was she to have known he didn't like talking about his work? Really, this man was like a firework waiting to go off—and she had no idea what might ignite the touchpaper!

'Well, for one thing I've never seen any books written by Sam Barton,' she said gently. 'So I just assumed that you must have a pseudonym. I apologise if I was wrong about that, but you don't give the impression you would welcome the publicity that can often follow a popular author,' she concluded lamely.

Lamely because the continuing cold intensity of his dark green gaze was completely unnerving, causing

Crys to give an involuntary shiver, despite the warmth from the Aga.

What had she said, for goodness' sake? No one had told her that this man's writing career was supposed to be a secret!

The ringing of the telephone cut through the icy silence.

Much to Crys's relief. With any luck, it would be Molly again. And, if it was, this time she intended being allowed to talk to her friend.

She found herself counting the number of rings before they suddenly ended, sighing with relief when it instantly began to ring again. It *was* Molly!

Sam shot Crys a derisive glance as he stood up to answer the telephone.

Obviously her relief at the interruption must have been evident on her face. Well, could she help it if her face tended to be a mirror reflection of her emotions?

'Caroline!' Sam said dryly into the receiver, dark brows raised mockingly as he looked across at Crys and saw her disappointment that the caller wasn't Molly, after all.

Crys instantly looked away, irritated at once again being the focus of this man's disdain. What did he do for entertainment when he hadn't got her to laugh at? she wondered disgruntledly.

And who was Caroline? Crys mused as she busied herself by standing up to remove the used plates from the table. She had to be a close friend from the warmth she could now hear in his voice as he spoke to the other woman. Also, the woman knew the code for getting Sam to answer a call. So perhaps he didn't spend all his time here alone—apart from sporadic visits from Molly, that was—after all?

It figured, really. He was an attractive single man of thirty-eight. It would be more unusual for him not to have a female friend, in the circumstances. *That* would be taking his hermit-like existence too far!

Crys found herself wondering, as she deliberately blocked out the soft murmurings behind her and finely sliced the carrots, what this Caroline was like. Not that it was any of her business, but it would be interesting, nonetheless, to know what sort of woman could manage to attract this ultra-critical man. A woman with extreme tolerance if she could cope with Sam's sudden mood swings!

'Perhaps you would care to share the joke?'

Crys gave a guilty start at being caught unawares—yet again! Smiling to herself, no less. Really, this man moved with such a cat-like tread it was completely unnerving to find him suddenly standing beside her. As he was now…

'No joke,' she answered him briskly, moving slightly away from him. 'My thoughts were miles away, giving you the privacy to—to enjoy your call.'

'Good of you,' he drawled.

Angry colour brightened her cheeks at his obvious sarcasm. 'I thought so,' she snapped back, eyes flashing.

'I just said so, didn't I?' he dismissed irritably. 'Will the main course be long?'

'Fifteen minutes or so?'

'Fine.' He nodded. 'I just have a couple of things to do first.' He turned abruptly on his heel and left the room.

Crys visibly wilted after he had gone, leaning back

against one of the kitchen units. Well, at least the telephone call had interrupted what had developed into a rather tense conversation—even if it hadn't been Molly, after all.

So much for the relaxing week in Yorkshire that Molly had promised her!

The most she could hope for at the moment, it seemed, was not to venture onto any more subjects—innocently or otherwise—that might prove explosive. The problem with that was she had no idea what those subjects might be.

And so she did what she always did when she was worried or disturbed—she cooked. It didn't take very long to find ingredients and whip up a creamy chocolate dessert, and she was just placing it in the fridge to cool when the telephone began to ring again.

So much for the recluse theory; this was the third telephone call Sam had received in the last few hours!

She listened to the rings, counting them without even realising she was doing it. One, two, three—right the way up to twelve. Then they ended abruptly. Before the ringing started again.

So it was a family member calling. Or another female friend, she acknowledged ruefully.

Except...the telephone just continued to ring. Wherever Sam was, he obviously either hadn't heard the telephone or wasn't in a position to answer it.

What should she do now? She knew without even asking that Sam would be furious if she were to answer his call. But she couldn't just let the thing continue to ring, either. It might be a family member checking up to make sure Sam was okay, and when he didn't answer—

'Leave it!' he ordered harshly as he entered the kitchen just as Crys was about to pick up the receiver.

Crys removed her hand as if the receiver had just burnt her, moving hastily out of his way as he moved to answer the call himself.

'This is ridiculous,' Crys muttered to herself as she busied herself serving up the vegetables to accompany the beef. She had only been about to answer the telephone, for goodness' sake; she hadn't been caught rifling through the man's personal papers! But from the way he had behaved, the fury in his face when he'd glared at her before snatching up the receiver himself, she might just as well have been!

It was no good; she simply couldn't stay here with this—

'Molly would like to speak to you.'

Crys looked up accusingly. Molly! After all that fuss, Molly was on the telephone!

Crys gave Sam an exasperated look as she moved to take the receiver from him, taking two calming breaths before lightly greeting her friend.

'You made it!' Molly came back happily. 'What do you think of Falcon House?' she added mischievously.

With Sam standing only feet away from her she wasn't really in a position to say! 'Interesting,' Crys replied non-committally.

Molly gave a gleeful laugh. 'I would ask what you think of Sam, too—but I have a feeling you would probably give me the same answer!'

'You would probably be right,' Crys answered awkwardly, very aware that the brooding Sam was still in the kitchen.

'He isn't doing his growly bear act, is he?' Molly

sobered worriedly. 'He promised me faithfully that he would behave himself,' she added exasperatedly.

'Your brother has been very welcoming,' Crys assured her, not quite truthfully. Sam's initial reaction to her had been antagonistic, to say the least, but he had been polite, if not exactly gracious, once he'd realised she was Molly's friend Crys. Besides, she had no intention of confiding the real situation to Molly over the telephone like this. Maybe she and Molly could have a laugh over it together once her friend arrived. *When* she arrived…

'Look, I'm really sorry I wasn't there to greet you when you arrived.' Molly seemed to pick up on some of Crys's thoughts. 'I'm flying back to London tomorrow night, and then up to Yorkshire the following morning. Do you think you'll be able to cope with Sam on your own until then?'

She would have to, wouldn't she?

Although a brief glance at Sam, his expression challenging as he confidently met her gaze, told her it wasn't going to be easy!

CHAPTER FIVE

'DID your mother ever tell you that the way to a man's heart is through his stomach?' Sam drawled self-derisively as he looked up and saw her watching his enjoyment of the portion of fillet of beef and roasted vegetables she had placed before him minutes earlier.

Crys had set about serving their meal once she'd finished talking to Molly, having no intention of sharing the subject of that brief conversation with Sam, even though the brooding intensity of his gaze as he'd watched her frowningly had told her that he might like to know.

She sipped the red wine he had poured to accompany their second course, wondering how her low-level tolerance of alcohol was going to cope after months of not drinking at all. She had only ever drunk wine to be sociable, and now that she had no one to be social with...

Which begged the question, she realised belatedly—why had she suggested that they drink wine with their meal at all?

Because, after months of feeling slightly estranged from people, she had craved some semblance of normality? To sit down and enjoy a meal with another human being, to talk of nothing in particular while they sipped their wine and ate their food? Perhaps. But the person you were with had to want that same sense of normality too—and she already knew there was nothing normal about Sam's way of life! He was more reclusive than she had become—and, unlike her, he seemed to enjoy it!

'My mother might have told me that,' Crys answered finally, 'but doesn't the man have to have a heart to begin with for that to be true?'

Coming from any other man, his comment about a man's heart would have sounded flirtatious, but from Sam it just sounded sarcastic. As she was sure it was!

The humour left his eyes, the humourless smile fading to cold implacability. 'The inference being that it doesn't matter in my case because I don't have one?' he bit out icily.

Crys shook her head wearily. 'There was no inference,' she sighed. 'I was merely answering like with like. Obviously a mistake on my part. I'm sorry.'

'No,' Sam replied hardly, after several long minutes of silence. 'I'm the one who's sorry. It's just—I'm not used—I'm not giving you too easy a time of it, am I?' he acknowledged.

'No, you're not,' Crys agreed evenly. 'But then why should you? You've had your privacy unexpectedly invaded by a complete stranger; I'm not sure I would be too happy about that either, if the situation were reversed.' Although she couldn't for the life of her think of any situation where Sam might turn up on her doorstep expecting a bed for the night!

'That isn't quite true,' he disagreed. 'I *was* expecting you—'

'But not on my own,' Crys reasoned gently. 'You thought Molly would be here too, and you certainly weren't expecting to have to play host to me in the way that you have.'

He drew in a ragged breath, before slowly letting

it out again. 'How about if you and I start again, Crystal—? I've just realised Molly didn't even tell me your surname!' he said. 'I'm sure she had better manners than this when she was a youngster!' He looked at Crys expectantly.

She hesitated. It wasn't that she didn't want to tell him her surname, just a question of which one... Webber or James?

Fifteen months ago, when she'd married James, she had changed her surname to his. In fact it had been a laughing point between them from their first intro- duction that her surname was the same as his Christian name. But until her marriage—and she still used it when dealing with some aspects of her life— her name had been Crystal James.

'Webber,' she supplied huskily. 'My name is Crystal Webber,' she added more firmly, hoping she was strong enough to cope with this. It had been a year, after all... 'Mrs Crystal Webber,' she elaborated pointedly.

'Webber...' Sam repeated softly. 'As in James Webber, the interior designer?'

Crys nodded. 'As in James Webber, the interior designer.'

Damn it, she wasn't strong enough, she realised, as her vision suddenly became misty with the tears that never seemed to be far from the surface nowadays.

'Hell, I'm sorry! I had no idea! What an idiot—'

'It's all right,' Crys assured him shakily, blinking back those sudden tears. 'I realise I should have told you earlier, when I guessed James had worked on the house, but I—'

'You don't have to tell me anything,' Sam cut in. 'But Molly should have warned me—'

'No, she shouldn't,' Crys defended wearily. 'What is there to tell, after all? I was married, and my husband—my husband died,' she concluded, surprised at how difficult it still was to say that word.

Sam looked at the gold wedding band that loosely encircled the third finger of her left hand. 'I hadn't even noticed you were wearing that.' He shook his head self-disgustedly.

'I've told you, it doesn't matter,' Crys hastened to assure him, wishing they could just change the subject; this one was proving far too painful.

Sam looked as if he might like to argue that point, but another glance at the paleness of her face had him nodding abruptly. 'Shall we start again then, Crystal?'

What was the point? She would be here for such a short time. Their paths would never cross again, she was sure. But perhaps for Molly's sake...

'Of course,' she accepted smoothly. 'Now, please do continue with your meal before it spoils,' she encouraged briskly. 'Where's Merlin, by the way?' She opted for a more neutral conversational subject, very aware of the fact that, although Sam had slowly recommenced eating his food, the intensity of his enigmatic gaze still rested on her.

'I thought it best to leave him outside for the moment,' Sam explained. 'That's where I went earlier—outside to feed him.'

'Please don't leave him outside on my account.' It was still damp and foggy out there—cold, too. 'I'm sure he'll quickly realise I pose no threat to either of you if he's allowed back inside,' she ventured dryly.

'I wouldn't be too sure about that,' Sam returned gruffly.

Crys looked at him sharply, her frown quizzical as

she came up against the shutter he kept closed over his emotions. Exactly what did he mean by that last remark?

Again, from any other man it might have sounded flirtatious, but coming from Sam—

She smiled, suddenly realising exactly what he had meant, and guessed that his compassion encompassed more than stray dogs. 'Did you take in injured birds and animals when you were a little boy, too?' she prompted knowingly.

'Did I—? What on earth are you talking about, Crystal?' Sam frowned darkly, again using her full name.

She sobered, shaking her head. 'Don't feel sorry for me, Sam,' she told him stiffly. 'Pity is an emotion I cannot abide!' And that included self-pity.

She had had six wonderful months with James— three of them as his wife; that was more than a lot of people ever had!

She stood up abruptly, picking up her plate to tip the half-eaten food into the bin. But she gasped in surprise as her arm was suddenly grasped and she was spun round to face a furious Sam as he glared down at her.

'I don't feel pity for you, Crystal,' he grated. 'And don't even attempt to tell me what I can and can't do!' he ground out angrily.

She blinked dazedly. 'But I wasn't—'

'Yes, you were, damn you!' he corrected, his face dark with fury. 'You— Oh, to hell with it!' he exclaimed, before his head lowered and his mouth took fierce possession of hers.

Crys was so stunned by the unexpectedness of his actions that for a few brief moments she stood unmoving in the tight band of his arms, the slenderness of her body crushed against the hardness of his as he very thoroughly kissed her.

So thoroughly, in fact, that she felt a long-forgotten stirring of desire. Heat, like molten lava, moved slowly into her body and it felt as if the ice in her heart was melting.

As, indeed, it probably was, she acknowledged with a choked cry. All warmth, all desire, had died with James. But this man, an admitted enigma, *couldn't* be the one to begin to heal her battered emotions!

She wrenched her mouth away from Sam's. 'Stop it!' she cried fiercely as she stared up at him in complete disbelief at what had just happened. 'Just stop it!' she repeated brokenly.

A humourless smile quirked the hardness of his mouth, although he made no move to release her. 'I thought I already had,' he murmured huskily.

Crys was breathing hard in her agitation. 'Let me go,' she told him coldly and pushed his arms away from her. 'I don't know what sort of woman you think I am, Sam, but—'

'I don't think you're any 'sort' of woman, Crystal,' he told her firmly.

'I am not a desperate widow in need of a quick romp—'

'I advise you to stop right there, Crystal.' Sam interrupted her, a nerve pulsing in the hardness of his jaw as he stepped away from her. 'I kissed you. I didn't, by word or intimation, give the impression that I expected that kiss to culminate in a trip to the bedroom. Perhaps next time it might be better to wait until you're asked!'

'Next time?' she gasped incredulously, her body trembling with reaction to this highly charged emotional scene.

His mouth twisted derisively. 'I wasn't necessarily implying it would be with me,' he replied scathingly. 'But, then again, you just never know...' he drawled, before striding confidently from the room.

She knew! There was no way on this earth that Sam Barton was ever going to kiss her again, let alone— let alone—

Crys sat down abruptly on one of the kitchen chairs, absolutely stunned by what had just happened, her lips still tingling, the blood singing hotly through her veins.

How could she have allowed herself to be kissed by that cold, arrogant, anti-social—?

That wasn't being quite fair to herself, Crys acknowledged heavily as her pulse began to slow, her head to clear. She hadn't exactly allowed Sam to kiss her; she had just been too surprised at the time to stop him.

Sam Barton, of all men. A man so unlike her late husband that they were like night and day. Storm and sunshine. James had been five feet ten in height—at least six inches shorter than this man—and blonde and blue-eyed, a smile never far from his lips... Whereas Sam, with his dark, brooding looks, didn't act as if he knew what laughter was!

She—

'Say hello to the nice lady, Merlin,' Sam drawled as he came back into the kitchen, the faithful hound now at his side, having obviously taken her at her word about bringing Merlin back in. 'I doubt he'll try to take a bite out of you,' he told Crys scathingly as she watched the dog warily as he slowly approached her. 'There isn't enough of you to give him a halfway decent meal!' he added insultingly.

Colour heightened her cheeks as she realised he was being deliberately insulting. Although, in the circumstances, that was probably better than him being nice to her!

'Hello, Merlin,' she greeted cheerily, holding out her hand for him to sniff. The dog's huge slavering mouth, with its vicious-looking teeth, didn't exactly give her any confidence in Sam's opinion!

'Animals are more apt to attack when they sense your fear of them,' Sam observed.

It wasn't only animals that did that, Crys conceded ruefully. Although she wasn't frightened of Sam—just found him totally unfathomable. Even more so now.

For a brief time, after he knew of her bereavement, he had seemed filled with compassion for her; she had no idea how that emotion had been turned into the searing passion with which he had then proceeded to kiss her!

'Good boy,' she told Merlin as he gave a tentative lick of her hand. 'Even if it is the smell of beef that you're coveting,' she added humorously.

'Don't be so disparaging about your own personal charm,' Sam said. 'It may be a little rusty from misuse, but I can assure you it's still there!'

Crys gave a troubled frown as she looked up at him. She didn't want to be told that she was still an attractive woman. Especially by Sam, she admitted to herself.

She had expected to spend a quietly reflective week in Yorkshire, to enjoy getting to know Molly again, and hadn't really given her friend's brother a lot of thought when she'd accepted Molly's invitation. She had assumed, if she had thought of him at all, that he would be busy with his own life—that the two women would probably see little of him, would make their own entertainment. Perhaps if Molly had arrived at the same time as Crys, as she had originally said she was going to, that might have been the case...

Only might have been, Crys accepted—because, having now met Sam, she doubted it would ever be possible to be just socially polite to him! She had quickly learnt that he was a man who provoked strong emotions: awareness and wariness, love and hate— Love...?

Crys doubted very much that any woman would ever find it easy to love such a mercurial man; he was far too uncomfortable to be around for any length of time. In fact, she was starting to feel quite sorry for the absent Caroline!

'I'm starting to dislike that enigmatic little smile of yours,' Sam rasped suddenly.

She blinked, focusing on him with effort as she straightened from stroking Merlin. 'I'm sorry...?'

Sam grimaced. 'You have a way of smiling to yourself as if you know a private joke you don't intend sharing with anyone.'

She certainly didn't intend sharing her thoughts of a few minutes ago with this man! 'Actually, I think I'm just tired.' She affected a yawn. 'Would you mind very much if I had an early night?' The last was said out of politeness only; she intended evading this man's company for the rest of the evening no matter what he might have to say on the matter. And all day tomorrow too, if she could manage it!

Sam's grimace deepened—as if he were well aware of her plans! 'Be my guest,' he murmured derisively. 'Just leave all of this for me to clear away.' His gaze encompassed the remains from their meal. 'It's the least I can do after you cooked for the two of us.'

She smiled. 'There's dessert in the fridge, if you're interested.'

'Thanks,' he accepted non-committally. 'There's a library full of books—second door on the right out of here—if you want to take a book up to bed with you,' he added with rather more politeness. 'There's even a selection of those murder-mysteries you enjoy!'

'Thank you.' Crys accepted in the same manner—although it was a little late in the day for this sort of politeness between the two of them. 'Will Merlin be okay now if I stand up to leave?' The dog was now stretched out in the warmth in front of the Aga, but as she already knew he could move very quickly if he chose to, despite his size.

'Try it and see,' Sam suggested unhelpfully.

He really was the most provoking—

Oh, damn him; no doubt if Merlin did take a flying leap at her Sam would be able to stop him before his teeth actually made contact with any part of her! If he chose to...

As it happened, apart from a twitch of one ear, Merlin didn't move as she stood up, although his pale gaze followed her movement across the room. She didn't even glance at Sam to see what his expression was like as she left the kitchen!

Second door on the right, he had said his library was—

Wow! As Crys opened the appropriate door she knew she had never seen so many books in one place.

Outside of a public library, that was. The four walls had bookcases from floor to ceiling, every shelf full, and there were several piles of books about the room too, because there was no more room to house them. Sam must be an incredibly fast reader; it would take her a lifetime to read all these books.

Eclectic, too, she discovered as she perused the shelves. There was everything here, from botany to astronomy. The fiction section was incredible too, from sagas to those mysteries he had mentioned.

Without even being consciously aware of it, she gravitated towards the cookery book section, choosing one at random from the large selection; reading other people's recipes had always relaxed her. And she definitely needed relaxing this evening!

The house was strangely quiet as she moved up the wide staircase, eerily so, despite the light given off by the chandelier overhead. She gave an involuntary shiver as she reached the gallery at the top of the stairs. The hallways were dark up here, and had her wondering exactly how many rooms there were in this mausoleum. More to the point, how many of them were habitable?

Not that it mattered particularly; she had no intention of going exploring!

'I forgot to tell you—if I'm not here when you come down in the morning, just help yourself to breakfast.'

She hadn't even been aware of Sam standing at the bottom of the stairs until he spoke to her, and turned sharply to look at him over the oak banister. 'Are you going out?' she enquired. Somehow, the thought of being left alone here in this huge barn of a house, even for a short time, wasn't a pleasant one. Even the company of the obnoxious Sam would be preferable to that, she realised.

He shrugged broad shoulders. 'I usually take Merlin for a run out on the moors first thing in the morning.'

Of course; a huge dog like Merlin would need a lot of exercise. 'I could always come with you,' she said quickly—and as quickly regretted it; she was hoping to avoid Sam's company tomorrow, not deliberately court it!

'You could,' he acknowledged dryly, but the mocking expression on his face told her that he was well aware of her earlier plan as regarded tomorrow. 'Have you brought any walking boots with you?'

As it happened, yes, she had. She hadn't been sure what Molly's plans were for this week, and as such she had tried to cover all contingencies. Including walking on the moors…

But not with Sam. The man was too probing, too personal, too—

'If you have, I'll be leaving here about seven-thirty. If you're interested,' he bit out with cold dismissal of her delay in replying.

He was just too everything! Crys concluded irritably. The uninterest in his tone just now had clearly told her that he didn't care whether she accompanied him in the morning or not—he was going out walking at seven-thirty anyway.

And why not? Wasn't that behaviour exactly what she had been expecting from Molly's brother in the first place? Really, this house seemed to be having some strange sort of effect on her; she certainly wasn't usually this contrary!

'Thank you,' she accepted evenly. 'Goodnight, Sam,' she added huskily.

'Crystal.' He nodded tersely before turning sharply on his heel and going back to the kitchen, the door closing behind him with a decisive click.

Crys paused as she heard the soft murmur of his voice, guessing that Merlin was the recipient of his one-sided conversation—but she was no doubt the subject of it. Sam was probably telling the dog about the complete contrariness of women, how they didn't know from one minute to the next what it was they wanted! But he would be wrong about the complete part of that statement; there was one thing Crys felt very clear on—she did not want a repeat of that kiss they had shared earlier!

She could still feel the force of that kiss. The warmth that had briefly coursed through her veins. Her own response—no matter how brief...

CHAPTER SIX

'WAS Merlin sleeping outside my bedroom last night as a way of making sure I stayed in there, or to be protective?'

Not that Crys really needed an answer to her question—she was already sure that it was the former!

She had had the shock of her life when, during the night, feeling in need of a hot drink to help with her sleeplessness, she had opened her bedroom door only to find Merlin sprawled across the doorway outside. He had merely opened one eye and looked up at her, but it had been enough for Crys to decide that a hot drink wasn't so necessary after all, before beating a hasty retreat back inside her bedroom, closing the door firmly behind her.

Sleep had been even less likely after that unexpected encounter with the Irish Wolfhound. She'd been aware by the snuffling and muffled movements on the other side of the door that the dog was making himself comfortable once again after being so rudely disturbed.

Consequently, her lack of sleep, and her irritation at having that guard placed outside her bedroom door, meant she was not in the best of moods this morning.

Sam stood up wordlessly to pour her a cup of coffee before placing it on the kitchen table in front of her. 'Not a morning person, hmm?' he taunted as he resumed his own seat.

Crys glared up at him, grey gaze accusing. 'It isn't

a question of that,' she snapped. 'And you didn't answer my question.'

Sam appeared not in the least bothered by her indignation. 'I thought you would feel safer with Merlin
sleeping outside your room.'

'Safer from whom?' she retorted; the only other
person in the house was Sam himself—and she was
sure Merlin wouldn't try to keep *him* out of her bedroom!

Sam still seemed not to be bothered. 'Just—safer.
I'm sorry if I was wrong.'

He wasn't sorry at all, Crys fumed inwardly as she
sipped at the reviving coffee. She would lay odds on
Sam always knowing exactly what he was doing—
and why!

'Do I take it from your appearance that you've decided to come for a walk with us this morning, after
all?' Sam remarked pleasantly, pointedly eyeing the
thick Aran sweater, black denims and heavy walking
shoes that she was wearing.

'Obviously,' she scorned, in no mood—despite the
fact that he had given her coffee—to forgive him for
placing that animal outside her bedroom the previous
night.

Because they both knew that Merlin had been keeping her in, not other people out!

She hadn't slept at all well since James had died a
year ago, and often found that a warm drink at one
or two o'clock in the morning would warm and relax
her enough for her to eventually be able to doze off
into a fitful sleep. Last night she hadn't even been
able to come out of her bedroom, let alone anything else!

'Obviously,' Sam echoed with soft derision, sipping his own coffee with clear enjoyment.

It was already seven-thirty, the time he had said he usually set off on his walk with Merlin, and yet he seemed in no hurry to be on his way. Yet another reason for Crys to feel annoyed with him—she had rushed her shower in order to be down on time!

'Shouldn't we be going?' she eventually prompted impatiently. Her sweater was really much too warm to wear in the heat of the kitchen.

'There's no rush,' Sam said evenly. 'The moors aren't going to disappear if we don't arrive at a certain time.'

Besides which, he was probably enjoying watching her sweat—glow, she corrected, as she recalled her defence of yesterday.

Crys stood up abruptly. 'I'll meet you outside when you're ready,' she announced irritably; the fresh air would probably do her good.

'Fine,' Sam agreed, before continuing to sip his coffee with that same infuriating slowness.

She was right about the air being fresh outside—it was bitterly cold, the wind cutting into her with the sharpness of a knife. But at least the fog had cleared this morning, giving her a better view of her surroundings.

If anything, the castle itself looked even more disreputable in the bright light of day, that air of decay and neglect even more noticeable. But it was only a façade, she reminded herself; the interior—parts of it, at least—was luxurious in the extreme.

Her boots crunched on the gravel as she walked out through the archway into the overgrown grounds that reached all the way to the boundary of the dis-used moat.

Except for the obvious mound of fresh earth that now edged the small orchard...

Sam might not be in any sort of hurry to leave for their walk, but he must have been up long enough to finish burying the dead dog he had found the day before.

Crys felt some of her overnight irritation leave her as she acknowledged the caring that had gone into this small service for a stray dog. As Sam had pointed out the afternoon before, the earth was frozen solid, and had been for some while, and it must have been back-breaking work digging that grave.

Amazing. Every time she decided that Sam was the most selfish individual she had ever met, he did some-thing that knocked that theory completely off-balance. And, of course—remembering the way he had kissed her the evening before—vice versa!

'Ready?'

She turned sharply to find Sam standing next to a disreputable-looking Land Rover she hadn't noticed parked next to the castle, a panting Merlin already ensconced in the back.

'Ready,' she agreed briskly, her gaze not quite meeting Sam's as she climbed into the vehicle beside him, remembering all too clearly the way he had kissed her the previous evening.

Perhaps too clearly...?

And why not? No man had kissed her since James had died; she was bound to feel a little unsettled when one did!

Was she protesting too much?

Maybe, she acknowledged self-derisively, but she

was still a little surprised at the fact that Sam had
kissed her at all.

There was nothing in his own manner to say he
remembered that kiss; he was completely silent on the
drive out onto the moors, and more occupied with
releasing Merlin from the back of the vehicle than
with Crys's comfort once they reached the spot he
had chosen for their walk.

Not that Crys was too concerned with what Sam
was doing. She was completely enraptured as she got
out of the vehicle by the rugged beauty of her surroundings, standing on a hilltop to gaze out across
land that seemed completely uninhabited by anyone
but Sam and herself.

Some people, she knew, thought the Yorkshire
moors were bleak and unwelcoming. But as she gazed
across all the untouched hills and valleys Crys felt a
lifting of her heart, a happiness she hadn't known for
a very long time at just being alive.

'It's got to you,' Sam said with some surprise.

Crys turned to look at him, her eyes glowing with
inner peace. 'It's just so beautiful.' She flung out her
arms to encompass all the grandeur of their surroundings.

'Shh, don't tell everyone!' Sam whispered. 'It's the
best-kept secret in Yorkshire!'

She laughed, her earlier irritability completely forgotten as they set off at a brisk pace in Merlin's wake,
the dog having already run off in search of rabbits,
real or imagined.

'What did you mean about it getting to me?' Crys
ventured lightly after they had been walking in companionable silence for some time.

Sam shrugged broad shoulders beneath the heavy

black sweater he wore to combat the cold wind. 'The Yorkshire moors are a place you either love or hate,' he responded.

'But you love them?' Crys ventured.

'And so, it appears, do you.' Once again there was that surprised note in his voice.

She gave him a sideways glance. He strode beside her with long, measured steps, allowing no quarter for her shorter legs. And she didn't want him to either, enjoying the briskness of the pace, feeling as if the clean Yorkshire air was reaching into her very veins. And as it did so it seemed to cleanse away all the pain and loneliness she had known this last year...

She tilted her head questioningly. 'Why did you think I wouldn't't?' It was perfectly obvious to her that was exactly what he had thought.

He hesitated for a moment. 'Molly is a town person. She likes to be around people, go to the theatre— when she isn't appearing at one! I just thought, as the two of you are such good friends... Maybe I was wrong. Again,' he added dryly, glancing at her with those mesmerising green eyes. 'I thought I had better say it before you did,' he explained self-derisively.

'I wouldn't have dared!' she came back teasingly.

Sam laughed softly. 'Oh, I think you might.'

Perhaps. But it was really too glorious a morning to argue or be at odds with anyone. Even the infuriatating Sam. At this particular moment nothing else seemed important but the still perfection of the day.

Sam seemed captured by the mood too, once again lapsing into a companionable silence. Which suited Crys perfectly; she just wanted to be left alone with her thoughts, to drink in as much of this cleansing air as she possibly could.

It was almost eleven o'clock by the time they returned to Falcon House, but Crys's earlier euphoria remained with her. She was feeling curiously at peace with the world. Even Sam!

'You're doing it again!' He frowned at her as he unlocked the back door and they went straight into the kitchen.

'Sorry?' She turned from filling up the kettle for a much-needed cup of tea.

'The enigmatic smile,' he explained irritably.

Her smile turned to a grin. 'Referring back to your comment last night—there's one thing my mother *did* tell me,' she said. '''Never let a man know all your thoughts; that way you always keep him guessing''!'

'No chance of anything else where you're concerned!' he said with mock disgust. 'Do your parents live in London too?'

Her smile disappeared abruptly, some of her gladness in the day evaporating too. 'My parents were both killed in a car crash six months ago,' she revealed as she turned away to busy herself with making the tea.

She heard him draw in a sharp breath behind her, followed by complete silence.

It was unfortunate Sam had chosen to ask her that particular question at this time, but there was no other way she could answer it except honestly. Now she didn't know what else to say—had no way of alleviating the sudden awkwardness of the moment. It—

She stiffened as strong arms moved about her waist from behind, pulling her gently back against the hardness of Sam's chest, his cheek resting on the top of her head as he held her close against him.

Perhaps even then she might have managed to remain calm and unemotional, to maintain the control she had exercised so successfully over the last six months. Perhaps…if Sam had remained silent too.

But he didn't…

'You poor love,' he said huskily. 'Hell, I thought I had the monopoly on— Never mind that,' he grated quietly. 'No wonder you fainted last night when you realised I was out there digging a grave! It must have been the last thing you wanted to see. And all I could do was accuse you of being an over-imaginative female!' he concluded self-contemptuously.

'You couldn't possibly have known,' Crys replied huskily, already well aware that Molly had told her brother nothing of Crys's personal life. Something Crys much appreciated. Although she wasn't sure Sam looked at it in the same way…

'Just how have you managed to survive this last year?' He groaned disbelievingly.

She swallowed hard. 'Please! I—I really don't want to talk about it.' She shook her head determinedly. 'I just want—I so enjoyed our walk this morning!' she added protestingly.

She had doubly enjoyed it, because not only had she been surrounded by unspoilt beauty, but she had also not given one single thought to the pain of the last year!

'And now I've spoilt it for you,' Sam acknowledged heavily, his warm breath stirring the tendrils of hair at her temple.

'No! Not really,' she continued more calmly. 'I just—' She drew in a ragged breath. 'I've already told you how I feel about pity!'

'It isn't pity I feel, damn it!' he exclaimed, his arms tightening about the slenderness of her waist.

Well, she certainly didn't want to know about any other feelings he might have at this particular moment! 'I really don't want to talk about any of it,' she repeated determinedly, moving firmly out of his arms, deliberately not looking at him as she stepped away, knowing it would be her undoing if she did. 'Let's just have a cup of tea, hmm?'

'The panacea for all Englishmen!' he muttered derisively.

'And Englishwomen,' she amended.

'Tea will be fine,' he accepted.

'Do you take milk and sugar?' Perhaps if she talked of normal, everyday things, she could forget the conversation they had just had. And the fact that Sam had once again taken her in his arms!

'No sugar. Thanks,' he extended ruefully. 'I enjoyed our walk this morning, too, Crystal,' he said gruffly.

'Good,' she answered non-committally, aware that the air of tense awareness that had sprung up between them in the last few minutes hadn't completely gone away.

She did not want to be aware of Sam. Or of any other man, come to that. Hadn't she already suffered enough this last year?

Like Sam, she had wondered herself how she was going to survive after the second shocking blow of her parents' deaths six months ago. But it appeared it was true that you couldn't die of a broken heart.

Her parents had been her rock and support after James died, and when she'd received the telephone call about their fatal accident she hadn't believed she could possibly go on. But somehow she had, and it was times like the walk across the moors this morning

that made her believe there had to be a brighter future.
She had no idea what it would be, but had come to
accept that it was part of life's mystery. It appeared
that life went on whether you wanted it to or not.

'I'm doing it again, aren't I?' she admitted as she
looked up to find Sam scowling across the table at
her. 'There's nothing enigmatic about my smile,' she
assured him. 'I'm just amazed—and not a little
dazed!—by the turns my life has taken this last year.
I have no idea what could possibly happen next.'

'Don't you?' Sam asked softly, green gaze blazingly intense.

'Do you?' Crys returned lightly.

'Would any of us want to know, even if we could?'
he responded seriously.

This conversation had become altogether too seri-
ous to be comfortable, Crys decided firmly, changing
the subject. 'What would you like for lunch today?'

Sam looked at her searchingly for several long seconds before giving a barely perceptible nod of his
head in acknowledgement of her deliberate shift from
the seriousness of their conversation. 'For you not to
have to cook it, preferably,' he drawled. 'You didn't
come here to work. How about I take you out for
lunch? There's a halfway decent pub about a mile
from here that does okay meals.'

Crys frowned. Going out for a walk on the moors
with him was one thing. Going out to lunch with
him—almost like being on a date?—was something
else entirely. 'Don't you have some work to do? Or
something?' she added lamely.

'Not work. Or something,' he answered derisively.
'I've just finished working on my latest—project, so
I'm taking a few weeks' well-earned break.'

And, unfortunately, she had chosen to visit during one of those weeks. Wonderful.

'Just because Molly isn't here don't feel you have to entertain me—'

'Have I given the impression, so far, that politeness is one of my virtues?' he cut in dryly.

'No.' Crys chuckled ruefully.

'Well, then?' he prompted.

It was only lunch, after all. What was she so afraid of, for goodness' sake? Hadn't she already spent the whole of last night alone in the house with this man? What was so difficult about going out to lunch with him today?

She drew in a deep breath. 'Okay,' she accepted.

'That wasn't so difficult, now, was it?' Sam teased.

He didn't know the half of it! Socialising, on any scale, wasn't something she had done a lot of this last year, for obvious reasons, and if it hadn't been for her work she probably wouldn't have had any reason to leave the house at all. Even going out for a pub lunch was an adventure for her nowadays.

She stood up, her cup empty of tea. 'What time do you want to leave? I didn't have time to wash my hair before going out this morning.' She explained her need to know.

'About twelve-thirty should do it. Long enough?' He looked admiringly at the length of her silver-blonde hair.

'Perfect,' she accepted. 'Dress casual?'

'Dress casual,' Sam echoed as he sat back in his chair to smile up at her. 'You're more rusty at this than I am!'

More rusty at what? Crys wondered, even as she

felt a strange fluttering sensation in her chest when she frowningly returned his gaze.

Without that growth of beard covering half his face he really was a very attractive man, very tall and lithe—even that unfashionably long hair, so dark and silky, actually suited him. As for those all-seeing green eyes…!

Stop it, Crys, she ordered herself sternly. He was Molly's brother. Her unwilling host. The fact that he had now decided to be pleasant to her did not make him anything else.

'I'll see you at twelve-thirty,' she told him, before turning to leave the kitchen.

'I'm looking forward to it,' he said.

Crys kept on walking, only starting to breathe normally again once she was out in the hallway, the kitchen door firmly closed behind her.

She wasn't sure she didn't prefer Sam when he was being rude to her!

It certainly felt safer.

Safer…?

What a strange way of putting it…

CHAPTER SEVEN

'THANKS,' Crys smiled as she accepted the half pint of lager and lime Sam had placed on the table in front of her. The two of them were cosily ensconced in the lounge bar of the pub Sam had driven them to, and a log fire was burning merrily in the grate, adding to the warmth of the interior. 'You mentioned earlier that you've just finished your latest book?' she prompted interestedly as he sat down beside her.

She had decided, while washing and drying her hair, that it would be better for them to stick to un-emotive subjects in future—that it was those brief insights into her personal life that were creating an air of intimacy between them that just shouldn't exist.

Although Sam didn't look as if he found the subject she had just chosen in the least unemotive!

He was frowning grimly as he gazed down into his pint of beer, his mouth a thin, uncompromising line. Finally he looked up, green gaze glacial. 'No, I didn't say that,' he replied.

'But—'

'Crystal, where did you get the impression that I write books?' he continued.

It was Crys's turn to frown now. 'Molly mentioned that you're a writer—'

'But not of books.'

'Oh,' she replied. 'I just assumed—' She broke off, already knowing it wasn't a good idea to assume anything where this man was concerned. Or to ask him any personal questions he didn't want to answer—which meant all of them!

A more secretive man she had yet to meet. She had answered all the questions he asked her, personal or otherwise, but Sam had a way of not answering a question directly. In fact, she knew very little more about him now than she had before she arrived yesterday. Less, in fact—he wasn't even the author she had thought him to be then!

'I'm a screenwriter, Crystal.' He spoke sharply, as if he would rather not be having this conversation at all.

Which he probably wouldn't, she acknowledged. A screenwriter? Living in the wilds of Yorkshire? It seemed rather a long way away from films or television.

'That's your cue to say "How fascinating", or "How interesting",' Sam rasped with heavy sarcasm.

Crys's mouth closed with a snap as she realised she had been about to say the latter. Really, this man was so touchy. He took offence—and became offensive—before she had even had chance to say anything!

'When you really have no idea whether what I do is either of those things,' he continued scathingly.

That wasn't strictly accurate, but she could see by his expression that he wouldn't believe her if she was to claim otherwise. Besides, his tone was so derisory, the approach of a herd of wild elephants in her direction couldn't have made her come out with either of those comments now!

She would really have loved to talk to him about his work—might actually have surprised him with what she did know. Molly certainly never dismissed her interest so scornfully!

'I doubt you would do it if it wasn't,' Crys finally answered him lightly.

'Not true,' Sam responded. 'I have to do something to keep the wolf from the door.'

'Or to keep the wolf that you have indoors!' she came back wittily, wanting to dispel the sudden tension between them. Again!

There was no subject, it seemed, that didn't eventually elicit a defensive response from this man. It was like walking through a minefield!

'That too,' he agreed. 'Do you know what you're going to eat yet?' He looked at the menu that lay untouched on the table in front of her.

Conversation very definitely over!

She turned her attention to the menu; perhaps food would sweeten Sam's mood. Although she wouldn't count on it!

But she discovered fifteen minutes later, when their food was delivered to the table by a cheerfully middle-aged barmaid, it certainly should have done. Her steak and ale pie was delicious, the pastry melting in her mouth, and even the chips served with it were crisp on the outside and delectably creamy inside.

'It's the brisk Yorkshire air,' Sam murmured dryly as he saw the way she was eating her food with relish. 'A couple of weeks here and you would put on all the weight that you've lost!' he added with satisfaction.

A couple of weeks here, spent in Sam's dubious company, and she was more likely to be a nervous wreck!

She eyed him questioningly. 'What makes you think I've lost weight?'

'Oh, that's easy.' He paused in his enjoyment of the gammon steak he had ordered as his own meal. 'Your clothes, while being well-made and of obviously good quality, are all a little big on you. And your wedding ring slides down to your first knuckle,' he continued as she would have spoken. 'If you aren't careful it may just slide off altogether!'

He was right, of course. In fact, she had even considered taking off her wedding ring a couple of months ago, if only to have it made smaller, having been sure herself that one day it was just going to slide off her finger completely and be lost for ever. James might be lost to her, but she didn't want to lose her wedding ring too...

'Quite the Sherlock Holmes, aren't you?' she said wryly.

Sam shrugged. 'Just observant.'

'That must be helpful when you're—' She broke off as she realised she had returned to the taboo subject of his work. 'Accurate observation of others isn't one of my strong points, I'm afraid,' she said instead.

'Maybe not,' he conceded. 'But I'm sure you could tell me in great detail every ingredient that went into making the pie you're eating!'

'I probably could,' she agreed laughingly, knowing down to the last herb. 'How astute of you!'

'You said you're a chef,' he pointed out. 'It was a pretty safe thing to guess.'

Maybe, but she knew she was nowhere near as astute where he was concerned. Of course he kept up a guard over most of his thoughts and emotions, but even so...

'It's delicious,' she assured him lightly.

'As pub food goes, yes,' he agreed, resuming eating his own meal.

Crys, while continuing to eat herself, watched him surreptitiously from beneath lowered lashes. A well-educated voice, so he was obviously a learned man—moreover a man who was obviously used to eating in much more sophisticated surroundings than these. She couldn't help wondering—and far from the first time!—what could have induced him to take himself off to the wilds of Yorkshire, to cut himself off from all but his family. Or almost all, Crys amended as she remembered the woman, Caroline.

She had become intrigued by this man without even knowing it was happening, Crys realised with dismay, suddenly losing her appetite for the food in front of her. Sam was not a man it would be wise to like, let alone become intrigued by!

Which made it even more difficult for her later that evening, when, having enjoyed scrambled eggs and smoked salmon for their meal, Sam suggested they go into the sitting room and watch a video together to pass the evening.

What made it difficult was that the room, with its brown and gold décor, was cosily intimate, the fire Sam lit in the old-fashioned fireplace making it even more so. They might have been like any other couple settling down for a comfortable evening together!

Except Crys felt even less comfortable in Sam's company now than she had yesterday when she arrived.

What was happening to her?

She loved James, had loved him from the first moment she saw him, that love only increasing as the weeks passed and it became obvious he felt the same way about her.

And yet...

She had lied earlier, even to herself, when she'd claimed not to be an observant person where others were concerned. Because she was aware of Sam in a way she never had been with any other man. Including James? a traitorous little voice asked inside her head. She was aware of the dark hair that grew on Sam's wrists, that shadow on the squareness of his chin that told of his need to shave twice a day, of the clean smell of his over-long dark hair, of the litheness of his body, of the black ring that encircled the irises of his eyes and so deepened them to dark emerald. She was also aware of every movement he made.

Like now. Crys gave a small start of surprise as he came to sit beside her on the sofa, rather than in one of the two armchairs closer to the fire...

Merlin felt no such compunction, settling himself down on the hearth-rug, his nose buried in his paws as he closed his eyes to sleep.

Sam turned frowningly to Crys, his arm lying lightly across the back of the sofa. 'What's wrong, Crystal?'

She swallowed hard, wrapping her arms protectively about herself, not sure what was happening to her. Only aware that she didn't like it!

'I don't know what you mean,' she dismissed lightly.

He grimaced. 'You seem...edgy. Have I done something to upset you? Because if I have—'

'You haven't,' she assured him. He hadn't done anything. It was only she who suddenly felt such a muddle of emotions! 'I apologise if I'm less than good company. It's just that I—I'm a little tired, that's all,' she excused awkwardly. 'In fact—'

'It's too early to go to bed, Crystal.' He firmly overrode what she had been about to say. 'Especially alone,' he added quietly.

Coming on top of her so-recent acknowledgement of her complete awareness of Sam as a man, this was just too much. Crys's cheeks coloured heatedly.

'Besides,' Sam continued, 'your early night yesterday didn't do you any good if you felt the need to leave your bedroom in the middle of the night. I am sorry about that, by the way; I'll make sure I take Merlin to my bedroom tonight.'

Crys had no idea where Sam's bedroom was—and she didn't want to know, either! It was of absolutely no interest to her. Had no bearing whatsoever—

This was terrible! What on earth was happening to her? She was twenty-six years old, and, although her marriage to James had been her introduction to a physical relationship, she had been out with plenty of other men before she met him. It was just that none of them had affected her quite in the way that Sam did...

'What colour would you call this?' Sam moved the hand he had draped across the back of the sofa, picking up strands of her hair to run them silkily through his fingers.

'Blonde?' Crys returned stiffly, fighting the instinct she had to move away from those caressing fingers. She shouldn't be able to feel the warmth of those fingers just through her hair and yet she did—every nerve-ending, it seemed, sensitive to his touch!

He smiled, shaking his head, even as he continued to watch those silky strands as they moved across his fingers. 'White-gold is about as near as I can come to describing it. And that doesn't even come close!'

Crys just wished he would stop touching her hair, that she wasn't completely aware of the warmth of his breath against her cheek, of the faint smell of limes in the aftershave he wore.

'It doesn't come out of a bottle, if that's what you're implying,' she told him sharply. 'Ouch!' she complained as his fingers tightened about her hair, tugging on it slightly at the roots. 'I was only—'

'I know what you "were only", Crystal,' he returned. 'What concerns me is why.' He frowned grimly, those fingers now entwined only tightly enough about her hair to stop her moving away from him rather than hurt her. 'Does it disturb you to have me touching you like this?' he probed.

Disturb her! She could barely breathe and her body felt as if it were on fire, if that was what he meant!

'Of course not,' she denied, reaching up to release her hair from his grasp so that she could sit forward. 'I think it's completely uncalled for—and certainly hasn't been encouraged—but that doesn't mean—'

'It does disturb you,' Sam said incredulously, eyeing her speculatively now. 'Crystal—' He broke off as she stood up.

She rounded on him angrily. 'Why do you persist in calling me by my full name when everyone else calls me Crys?' she attacked, her whole body tense with emotion.

'Probably because I prefer not to consider myself as belonging to "everyone else",' he drawled dismissively.

'Rather arrogant of you, isn't it?' she returned scathingly, aware that she was being incredibly rude—but then, good manners had never been a particular part of her conversations with Sam!

'Maybe,' he conceded, watching her with some amusement now as he relaxed back on the sofa. 'But Crystal is too beautiful a name to be shortened to just Crys.' His mouth quirked with distaste for the abbreviation.

'Perhaps I consider Samuel to be a nicer name than Sam!' She was being completely childish now, she knew, but something inside kept driving her on. A part of her was desperate to antagonise him—at least she knew where she was with him when he was being cutting and arrogant!

'Perhaps you do,' he smiled, apparently—infuriatingly!—completely unperturbed by her outburst. 'And I'm sorry to disappoint you, but I'm afraid I was christened just Sam.'

She had just made a complete fool of herself, Crys realised. For no reason, it seemed. Because Sam wasn't in the least annoyed by her remarks. In fact he looked more amused than ever!

'Well, Just Sam,' she bit out tautly, 'I thought we were going to watch a video?'

'We are,' he agreed, still watching her thoughtfully, a faint frown-line between his eyes now. 'Crystal, why are you suddenly as jumpy as a newborn fawn?' he asked slowly.

Because that was how she felt! She was twenty-six, she had been married—very happily!—and yet the awareness she felt for Sam was completely new to her.

Perhaps it was the bracing Yorkshire air, after all. Perhaps all that good, clean air had intoxicated her. Because that was certainly how she felt: a little off-balance, her head buzzing, unable to put two coherent thoughts together.

'I thought, despite our rather rocky start yesterday, that we'd had a good day together,' Sam said in a slightly puzzled voice.

'We have! I have,' she corrected, unable to speak for Sam. 'It's just—' she broke off with a sigh.

Just what? she questioned herself impatiently. That she didn't see Sam as just Molly's brother? The man couldn't possibly be classed as 'just' anything—despite her earlier attempt at sarcasm concerning his name! He was a man like no other she had ever met. Or was ever likely to meet.

And she didn't like the fact that she felt that way.

It was disloyal to James, to the time they had had together, to their marriage, to their love. Physical attraction to another man—for she surely didn't know Sam well enough for it to be anything else!—was a betrayal of what she had shared with James. Wasn't it…?

'Crystal…?' Sam stood up too, his expression quizzical as he moved towards her.

She couldn't move! Her feet felt anchored to the carpeted floor, her legs leaden.

'Crystal, this is not a good idea,' he protested huskily.

She felt like a rabbit caught in the headlights of a car, completely motionless as she watched Sam's head slowly bend towards hers, as his arms moved strongly about the slenderness of her waist, his eyes wide open, his gaze meeting her widely startled one as his mouth claimed hers in a deeply searching kiss.

Crys gave a low sob in her throat even as her lips parted to receive that kiss, her eyes closing now, her

body suffused with warmth, her arms moving up instinctively to his shoulders.

'You are so beautiful…!' Sam groaned seconds
later, his lips moving warmly down the column of her
throat to the tempting hollow beneath.

At that moment she felt beautiful. Totally desirable.
Totally *alive*.

That was it, she suddenly realised. After feeling
emotionally dead for the last year, with everything
she did being done out of habit and routine rather than
any real desire to do it, Sam had made her feel alive
again…

'Crystal?' He raised his head to look at her now,
his gaze darkly searching as he seemed to sense her
total shock at this discovery of life—of love?—flow-
ing through her veins once more.

She swallowed hard, her own gaze fixed on the
sensuousness of his mouth. The mouth that had so
recently kissed her own. 'Sam, I don't want to talk.'

'Tell me what you do want?' he prompted.

She trembled slightly within the circle of his arms,
moistening dry lips with the tip of her tongue before
speaking. 'I want—'

'Hello-ee…? Is anyone home?'

Crys's second shock, at the sound of that suddenly
intrusive voice, was even deeper this time. All colour
left her cheeks and a look of total disorientation
clouded her features, her frown of confusion widening
as Sam's arms dropped from about her waist and he
stepped away from her.

Who—?

The door to the sitting room was suddenly flung
open, and a brightly smiling Molly was standing in
the doorway.

'Surprise!' she shouted happily, flinging her arms wide in greeting. 'I managed to get an early flight back from the States this morning.' She chattered excitedly as she came further into the room, throwing her scarf and gloves into a chair as she did so. 'A connecting flight up here, a hire car—and *voilà*, here I am!' She moved forward to clasp Crys in a bear-hug.

Here she was, Crys acknowledged numbly, her gaze briefly meeting Sam's over Molly's shoulder as the two women hugged. A private message passed between the two of them of how surprised Molly might have been. A few minutes later and Molly might have been very surprised indeed!

CHAPTER EIGHT

THANK goodness Molly seemed completely unaware of Crys's numbness as she turned to affectionately greet her brother, the brief respite giving Crys time to attempt to gather her scattered defences back together.

Which wasn't easy when she knew, but for Molly's unexpected arrival, she had been about to tell Sam that she wanted to make love with him!

She gave an inward groan of embarrassment, turning away to stare unseeingly at the fire, mortified at what she had almost done. How could she? Sam was a man who made no secret of the fact that he kept everyone but his close family firmly at bay. The fact that he had kissed her, told her she was beautiful, didn't change any of that.

What could she have been thinking of?

She hadn't been thinking at all, only feeling—that was the problem!

'Gosh, it's good to be here at last!' Molly flung off her coat. She was a short redhead, and the effervescence and warmth of her personality shone in her laughing brown eyes. 'So what have you two been up to today?' she prompted interestedly as she moved to warm her hands by the fire.

Crys couldn't even look in Sam's direction at that moment—wasn't sure he had even spoken since releasing her from his arms. Although she supposed he must have said something to Molly in greeting; her

friend certainly didn't look as if she suspected any
sort of atmosphere between the two of them—awkward or otherwise!

'This and that,' Crys answered awkwardly, instantly recognising that she had to pull herself together if Molly wasn't to quickly catch on to the fact
that there was something not quite right here, even if
she couldn't possibly guess what it was.

The last time Molly and Crys had met Crys had
been newly in mourning for James, and she was sure
that Molly was perfectly cognizant of her brother's
unsociability; the fact that Crys and Sam had somehow become attracted to each other wouldn't even
occur to her friend, Crys felt sure.

Thank goodness!

'We went for a long walk out on the moors this
morning.' Sam stepped capably into the breach left
by Crys's own inadequate reply to Molly's question.
'Then we went out for lunch. And this afternoon—'

'Stop!' Molly held up her hand, her smile bright.
'You're wearing me out just listening to you!' She
collapsed down onto the sofa Crys and Sam had so
recently vacated. 'I'm exhausted after all that travelling,' she confided wearily.

She didn't look exhausted, looking just as good as
she usually did—very smart in a pink polo-necked
jumper and burgundy-coloured trousers, her boots a
perfect match in colour. Molly had a beauty that
glowed from within, lighting up her classical features,
giving warmth to the softness of her brown eyes. It
was a quality that shone out of her when she was
acting.

'Can I get you anything to eat?' Crys offered
lightly. 'I'm sure, from experience, that you can't

have had anything in the least edible on the journey here!'

'Do you know what I would really like?' Molly grinned across at her. 'Some of your delicious pancakes with maple syrup and ice cream!'

'You've been in America too long, my girl.' Sam grimaced. 'Or else you're pregnant...?' he added controversially.

'Ha, ha, very funny,' Molly came back. 'Don't knock it until you've tried it!'

'Pregnancy, or pancakes and ice-cream?' Sam retorted wittily.

'Sam—'

'Pancakes and ice cream coming up.' Crys interrupted their sibling banter, glad of an excuse for leaving them to it and going through to the kitchen.

Escaping, more like, she berated herself as she left the room. But no matter how she tried she couldn't get away from the realisation that if Molly hadn't arrived when she did...!

But she had. And nothing had happened. Not really.

Only because she and Sam had been interrupted! that niggling little voice taunted inside her head.

She was getting a little tired of that voice. What was it anyway? Conscience? Or that other side of herself that was trying to break free, to put the past behind her and move on?

But she didn't want to move on! Did she...?

'Make that two for pancakes and ice cream.' Sam spoke softly from behind her, making Crys instantly drop the egg she had just taken from the fridge.

'Now look what you've made me do!' she exclaimed resentfully, her face bright red as she went down on her haunches to clear up the mess.

No one had made her do anything—Sam's appearance in the same room as herself was enough to rattle her nerves anew!

'Leave it!' Sam ordered, even as he reached down and clasped her arm, his grip like steel as he pulled her upright. 'We haven't finished our conversation,' he reminded her, his eyes deeply searching on the paleness of her face.

Crys glared at him. He didn't have to remind her—yes, he did! Sam was not a man who shied away from anything. Even embarrassing situations. Embarassing to her, that was...

'It's finished, Sam,' she told him flatly, the strength of her gaze determinedly meeting his, telling him with more than words that she wasn't just talking about their conversation.

He continued to look at her for several long seconds, his eyes narrowed censoriously. 'Coward,' he finally said disgustedly, releasing her abruptly.

'Possibly,' she bit out tautly, turning away. 'Thank goodness Molly arrived when she did, hmm?' she added disparagingly, once again turning her attention to the smashed egg on the floor.

'That's a matter of opinion,' he returned.

Crys glanced up at him. 'Isn't she going to think it rather odd if you just leave her to her own devices when she's only just arrived?'

'Possibly.' He scathingly repeated her own earlier comment. 'But then, I'm not here to entertain Molly!'

'Or me,' Crys pointed out, throwing soiled paper towels into the bin, studiously keeping her gaze averted from Sam. Aware, even as she did so, that part of her was still pulsing with the desire she had known so recently in his arms.

'You're more recreation than entertainment,' he came back caustically.

She had probably deserved that, Crys acknowledged heavily. 'The pancakes will be five minutes,' she told him pleasantly, refusing to rise to his obvious baiting.

Sam's eyes crinkled to steely slits. 'I'm not sure that I'm hungry any more,' he finally said slowly.

Crys turned impatiently. 'Make your mind up, Sam—either you do want pancakes or you don't.'

He drew in a harsh breath, a nerve pulsing in the hard set of his jaw. 'Contrary to what you might think—or say!—I consider our earlier conversation far from over, Crystal.'

She felt a nervous fluttering in her stomach at the threat behind his words. He intended returning to that conversation at a later time. Preferably when they wouldn't be disturbed, no doubt…

But none of that nervousness showed as she held a second egg up questioningly over the bowl of flour.

'Why not?' he demanded. 'Even if it isn't the right sense that's being fed!' he added derisively, before striding impatiently from the room.

Crys's breath left her in a shaky sigh as soon as he had gone, and she leant weakly against one of the kitchen units, closing her eyes with a groan.

What was she going to do?

She had thought, when Molly arrived, that the awkwardness of this situation would ease. But what had happened between Sam and herself a short time ago—and whatever that might be she still wasn't sure!—made that impossible. In fact, if anything, Molly's arrival had made things worse; there was no way Crys could make her excuses and leave when her friend had only just got here!

Even if that was what she most wanted to do!

Was she being cowardly by wanting to run away? Of course she was! But, at the same time, wasn't she right to feel that way? Her beloved husband had died a year ago, both her parents six months later; it would be sheer madness on her part to become emotionally involved with anyone ever again—and especially with a man like Sam.

Apart from Merlin, Sam lived a completely solitary life here, and if there were women in his life— Caroline?—then they weren't women who were actually allowed to *share* his life. Crys simply wasn't the kiss-and-move-on type. She never had been.

Which left nowhere to go for any sort of relationship between Sam and herself.

No, she had been right to call a halt when she did, she decided determinedly. Even if Sam didn't exactly agree with her! Once he had thought it through, he too would see the sense in—

'Gosh, it's good to be here at last!' Molly burst out enthusiastically as she came through to the kitchen, running her fingers through the heavy weight of her red hair. 'And to see you,' she added as she looked searchingly at Crys. 'How are things? Oh, don't worry, Sam has gone for a walk outside with Merlin,' she assured her as Crys glanced past her awkwardly.

'Things are fine,' Crys answered her friend dryly, lightly beating the batter for the pancakes as she waited for the oil to heat in the frying pan. 'The restaurant is doing well. I have a few weeks off from—'

'I wasn't talking about work, Crys,' her friend admonished, giving her arm a brief squeeze. 'I want to know how *you* are.'

Crys gave a rueful smile. 'Well, work is all I am at the moment.'

'Still?' Molly frowned. 'Crys, it's been over a year since—well, since—'

'Since James died,' Crys finished softly. 'You seem to have more trouble saying it than I do...' She looked at her friend searchingly.

Molly had attended James's funeral, and the two women had kept in touch by telephone afterwards. Molly had also appeared at the funeral of Crys's parents, some months later, but the two women hadn't met like this for a long time. Too long, Crys acknowledged slowly.

Molly had been friends with James long before she'd introduced him to Crys, and Crys had wondered for some time if she wasn't intruding on a romance between the two of them. But James had laughingly assured her that he and Molly had never felt that way about each other, that they had only ever been friends. Crys had no idea whether Molly had felt the same innocuous affection for James...

Molly looked a little uncomfortable now, chewing on her bottom lip. 'If you want to know the truth, Crys...' she began slowly.

Crys stiffened, not sure she did want to know the truth at this particular moment; she was still too raw from being in Sam's arms to cope with any more shocks—such as hearing that Molly had been in love with James all along!

Molly sighed. 'The thing is, I've always felt a little guilty. About James, I mean.' She grimaced.

'Guilty?' Crys repeated reluctantly.

'Mmm,' her friend murmured. 'But perhaps this isn't the time to talk about this…'

Perhaps it wasn't, but having now started on the subject…! 'It's okay with me, Molly,' Crys assured her.

'Well, you see— Hello again, Merlin.' Molly broke off laughingly as the hound bounded into the kitchen, jumping up at her and almost knocking her down with the enthusiasm of his greeting.

Where Merlin was, Crys knew that Sam wouldn't be far away. The dog rarely left his master's side— when he wasn't standing guard outside women's bedroom doors, that was!—but, even so, she had already tensed herself for the encounter when Sam strode into the kitchen seconds after Merlin.

His cold green gaze flickered over her briefly, before he turned his attention to his sister and the dog. 'Down, Merlin!' he commanded, and the animal instantly obeyed to wander over to watch Crys's activity at the Aga.

'Wouldn't it be heavenly if all males were that obedient?' Molly grinned.

Sam's mouth twisted humourlessly. 'My dear Molly, most of us are—in the appropriate circumstances!'

'Ha!' Molly snorted scathingly. 'I can guess what they might be!'

'How about you, Crystal?' Sam challenged as he made himself comfortable in one of the kitchen chairs. 'Can you guess too?'

Just as easily as Molly could! But, once again, his conversation really wasn't that of a polite host to a guest—moreover not his own guest, but his younger sister's. A fact Molly, one of the most astute people

Crys had ever met, wouldn't be ignorant of for long if Sam continued to behave in this familiar way.

'Could you lay the table for me?' Crys prompted briskly. The first pancake was almost ready for serving.

Green eyes openly laughed at her deliberate evasion. 'How many for?' Sam enquired as he stood up. 'Two or three?'

'Two—'

'Oh, do join us, Crys,' Molly encouraged eagerly. 'It will be something like the midnight feasts we used to enjoy at school, remember?' Her eyes glowed with memories of those nights when they'd used to sneak out of school to sit on the sea wall that edged the playing fields, with their tuck-boxes and cans of drink, believing they were being very daring in breaking the school rules.

'Yes—do join us, Crystal,' Sam echoed tauntingly, his task of preparing the table complete. 'Then the two of you can tell me exactly when it was you managed to get any schoolwork done!'

Molly wrinkled her nose at him. 'Oh, don't be such an old poop, Sam. Didn't you ever—? Oh, thanks, Crys; this looks wonderful!' she exclaimed as the plate containing her pancake, maple syrup and ice cream was placed on the table in front of her. 'Excuse me, Sam, but we'll have to continue this argument later; Crys's cooking is to die for!'

'Yours will be ready in a moment,' Crys told Sam softly as he seated himself opposite his sister at the table.

His confrontational gaze met hers head-on. 'I can wait,' he told her quietly.

She moved hurriedly back to the Aga. Like a frightened rabbit, she admonished herself. No, not really; she was just starting to feel slightly threatened from several areas. Molly seemed on the verge of some momentous confession—and it was one Crys was sure she didn't want to hear. As for Sam—! He just didn't like being thwarted, she decided, and by refusing to even discuss what had happened between them earlier he believed she was doing exactly that.

Well, he would just have to continue thinking that, because she had no intention of—

'Mmm, this is delicious!' Molly breathed ecstatically across the room. 'Worth every hour of travelling I've had to do today. Wait until you taste this, Sam; it's heavenly!'

'I've already tasted Crystal's cooking,' he came back tautly.

'What?' Molly gasped, almost choking on her second mouthful of pancake. 'You haven't been making her work since she got here?'

He shrugged unconcernedly. 'She didn't have anything else to do.'

Molly's eyes widened. 'But, Sam—'

'Your brother is quite right, Molly,' Crys interjected tautly, flicking Sam a cold glance as she did so. 'I was happy to be of some use.'

'But—'

'Here you are, Sam.' Crys firmly put the plate containing his pancake down on the table in front of him. 'Help yourself to the maple syrup and ice cream,' she invited, putting the jar and tub on the table next to him.

'Service seems to be slipping,' Sam came back derisively, giving a pointed look at Molly's prepared pancake.

'Sam, really!' Molly looked scandalised by the remark. 'You can't talk to Crys like that!'

'I thought I just did.' He looked completely unperturbed by the rebuke.

'Yes, but—'

'It really doesn't matter, Molly.' Crys shot her friend a warning look, in the process of preparing a much smaller pancake for herself, unwilling to have the label party-pooper hurled at her—which she was sure, in the mood he was in, Sam would lose no opportunity to do!

'Of course it matters.' Molly wasn't to be put off, still glaring at her brother.

'Crystal doesn't seem to have minded,' Sam dismissed. 'So why should you? Besides,' he added mockingly, 'she's a much better cook than you are!'

'Well, of course she is.' Molly sighed. 'Ordinarily people pay a lot of money to eat the food Crys has prepared, you ungrateful man, you,' she told Sam exasperatedly.

The spoonful of pancake on its way to Sam's mouth halted before it got there, and his gaze narrowed as he looked across the room at Crys. 'And why should people pay a lot of money to eat food Crystal has prepared?' he said slowly.

'Because she's *Crystal*, silly.' Molly's frustration deepened.

'I just called her that, didn't I?' Sam rasped.

'Yes, but—'

'For goodness' sake stop starting every sentence with "Yes, but",' Sam snapped impatiently.

Molly glared at him. 'Maybe I would if you stopped interrupting me!'

'I wouldn't need to keep interrupting you if you were making any sense,' Sam returned caustically.

'You—'

'Please!' Crys cut in soothingly, picking up her plate to join them at the table, choosing to sit down next to Molly rather than at the place Sam had set beside himself. 'Please don't argue on my account. I think what Molly is trying to say is that—'

'She's *Crystal*!' Molly cut in exasperatedly.

'You're starting to repeat yourself now,' Sam said.

'Of the London restaurant Crystal,' Molly explained. 'Of the television programme *Crystal's Cuisine*. For goodness' sake, Sam, you have one of her cookery books on your shelf in the library; I bought it for you myself last Christmas!'

Crys looked reluctantly at Sam from beneath lowered lashes, knowing that her reticence was warranted when she saw the intense dislike on his face as he looked back at her with accusing eyes.

If Molly thought she had done Crys any favours by informing her brother of exactly who 'Crystal' was—that she was a restaurant owner, bestselling author of cookery books, and television personality—then Molly could think again. Sam looked as if he would rather not be in the same room with her!

CHAPTER NINE

IN FACT, at that moment Sam suited his actions to his expression, putting down his spoon and fork, leaving his pancake untouched, and pushing his chair back noisily to get abruptly to his feet.

'If the two of you will excuse me,' he muttered tightly. 'I've just remembered some things I need to do.' Without waiting for either of them to answer he strode forcefully from the room, the faithful Merlin following at his heels.

'Well!' Molly exclaimed as she stared after him incredulously. 'What on earth is wrong with him?' She turned back to Crys.

'From the little I've come to know about your brother these last two days—which isn't a lot, I might add!—I would say he's had enough of chattering females for one evening,' Crys replied, knowing that was far from the full story but hoping that Molly would accept that version for the moment. Sam had really just wanted to remove himself from the presence of only one female—herself!

Molly shook her head. 'Has he been like this since you arrived yesterday?' She frowned her displeasure at the thought.

What on earth was Crys supposed to say in answer to that? Sam had been decidedly unwelcoming when she'd first arrived, but they had gone for a walk together this morning, and Sam had taken her out for lunch today too. It was the fact that they had been in

each other's arms only an hour ago that had changed
things between them. But she wasn't about to tell
Molly that!

'He's been fine,' Crys answered lightly. 'I don't
think he was too impressed with my resumé just now.
I also don't think it helped the situation that until I
actually arrived Sam was under the impression you
were bringing a man called Chris here with you!'

Molly shook her head impatiently. 'I gathered that
when I spoke to him on the telephone yesterday.
Honestly—men! They never listen to a word you say
to them!' She sighed. 'I've been talking to him about
my friend Crys for years!'

'So he told me,' Crys recalled dryly. 'But he obviously didn't make the connection between the two
when you asked if you could bring a guest here this
week.'

Her friend gave her a knowing look. 'He wasn't
rude to you when you got here yesterday, was he? I
know Sam isn't the easiest of men—'

'I told you, he was fine,' Crys reassured Molly,
thinking her friend's comment about Sam had to be
the understatement of the year! Sam was the most
prickly of men she had ever had the misfortune to
meet!

'I hope so,' Molly said slowly. 'I do so want the
two of you to get on.'

Crys looked at her friend. Was it her imagination
or was Molly's gaze suddenly evasive...? 'Molly,
what—?'

'There, now, my pancake is getting cold,' her
friend burst out petulantly, tucking into her food with
renewed gusto.

'I'll make you a fresh one,' Crys offered distractedly, the previous conversation far from over as far as she was concerned. 'Molly—'

'This will be fine,' the other woman assured her. 'I just can't believe that Sam didn't know who you are!' She gave another exasperated shake of her head.

'Why should he?' Crys made no effort to eat her own food—had only prepared it in the first place because she'd felt she ought to be sociable. But Sam obviously felt no such compunction, so why should she?

'Look, Crys, you may not own a television, but Sam certainly does; I can't believe he hasn't seen at least one of your programmes. You're into your third season, for goodness' sake!' Molly exclaimed.

It had been that recognition Crys had thought she would see when she'd taken her hat and scarf off here in the kitchen yesterday—the reaction she had been expecting. And had dreaded! Because she had come here for a complete holiday—away from the restaurant, recording television programmes, and the compiling of the books that went with those programmes. But it had been a recognition that just hadn't happened in Sam's case...

She gave a small smile. 'Somehow he doesn't strike me as a man who watches cookery programmes.'

'Maybe not,' Molly conceded grudgingly. 'But there are your books too. I told you, I gave him one last Christmas.'

'It was a nice thought, Molly, but I doubt Sam reads cookery books, either,' Crys teased. 'He probably just filed it away on a shelf in the library without even looking at it.'

'Then it was very ungrateful of him,' muttered a disgruntled Molly.

'Don't you think we're straying from the point a bit here?' Crys prompted gently.

Molly repressed a yawn as she blinked across at her. 'I'm sorry, but I'm afraid I've forgotten what the point was.' She gave an apologetic smile. 'I'm rather tired; it's been a very long day.'

Of course it had. Molly must have been travelling for hours. It was only that—

'I have to confess,' Molly said, 'I thought I had better rush back as soon as I could after talking to you on the telephone last night; you sounded a little stressed out.'

Crys pulled a face. 'I travelled most of yesterday myself,' she admitted.

Molly nodded. 'Then an early night probably won't do either of us any harm. I hope you don't mind? I'm a little jet-lagged, but I'm sure I'll be feeling more sociable tomorrow.'

'No, of course not,' Crys readily agreed. 'You go up. I'll clear away here,' she assured Molly as she made to start tidying the table.

Molly hesitated. 'Are you sure?'

'Positive,' Crys said, standing up. A few minutes to herself wouldn't come amiss either! 'You go up and have a relaxing bath or shower before crawling into your nice warm bed. I'm quite happy pottering about here.'

'You are a love!' Molly reached out and gave her one of her spontaneous hugs. 'It really is good to see you, Crys.' Molly held her at arm's length. 'I know we've talked on the telephone regularly, but it's been far too long since we got together like this,' she said wistfully.

Yes, it had. Oh, they both had heavy work schedules—Molly working in the States the last year, Crys caught up with her restaurant and recording television programmes—but after her interrupted conversation with Molly earlier she couldn't help wondering if that hadn't just been an excuse for their not meeting. Perhaps James was part of the reason the two women had not managed to meet? On Molly's part, at least...

Crys sincerely hoped not. It would be too awful if it turned out Molly had been in love with James all along—that her friend had actually lost him twice. Once to another woman and then to the cold inevitability of death.

Crys gave Molly's arm a squeeze. 'We'll have time for a long chat tomorrow.' She smiled encouragingly.

'Hmm.' Molly stepped back, giving another tired yawn. 'If I manage to get up at all, that is,' she admitted. 'Do you and Sam have any plans for tomorrow?'

Did she and Sam have any plans...? Crys wasn't sure she liked being grouped with Sam in that way!

'Of course not, silly,' she dismissed lightly. 'We were expecting you to arrive tomorrow anyway.' And even if they hadn't been Crys knew she would have done everything she could to avoid spending any time alone with Sam now. Tomorrow or any other time.

'Fine.' Molly nodded. 'I'll see you some time in the morning, then.' She smiled tiredly before leaving the room.

Presumably Molly knew in which room she would be spending the night. Even if she didn't, it certainly wasn't up to Crys to interfere. One thing she did know: it wasn't the double bedroom Sam had expected his sister to be sharing with a man!

Sam...

What was she going to do about him? If anything... She could just try pretending that none of today had happened. Although, after what Sam had said to her earlier, she had a feeling he wouldn't be willing to let it go as easily as that.

Which was rather silly of him, in the circumstances. She would be here for only a few more days—had promised the manager of her restaurant that she would be back in town by the weekend. Five more days; would she be able to stand it here with Sam for that length of time? One thing she did know. There was absolutely no future for a relationship of any sort between Sam and herself; she had her busy life in London, and Sam had his life here. And then there was Caroline...

But, no matter how much Crys might try to deny it, she had enjoyed those moments in Sam's arms—had felt truly alive for the first time in months. Since James had died, in fact.

Physical attraction? Was that it?

She couldn't say it was something she had ever experienced without love before, but there was always a first time for everything. Because she certainly wasn't in love with Sam!

Not only was he prickly, he was also arrogant, overbearing, rude, sarcastic—in fact, she would be hard put to find any good points about him.

He was kind to animals and sometimes to widows.

There was no doubting his compassion concerning the dog that had died. Or Merlin's complete devotion to him. There was also no denying that Sam had been kind to her, in his own way, since she had told him she was James's widow.

Okay, Crys accepted, so he was kind to animals and widows.

He also loved and cared about Molly. As Molly loved and cared for him.

She was talking herself into a corner here, Crys realised. She and Sam were as different as chalk and cheese, and let that be an end to it—

'I thought I might still find you here,' Sam said, so close behind her that Crys gave a nervous start of surprise, almost dropping the plate she had just picked up to remove from the table. 'You ought to get something done about that jumpiness of yours,' he advised.

Crys's eyes flashed deeply grey as she turned sharply to face him. 'Such as?' she challenged, deeply resenting his implication that she was a nervous wreck, knowing that it was only this man who caused her to react so violently.

He shrugged broad shoulders. 'I have no idea,' he drawled. 'But it can't be good for the profits of your restaurant business if you go around dropping plates all over the place!'

'But I didn't drop it.' She held the plate up intact. 'And my business is doing just fine, thank you—with or without my supposed jumpiness,' she told him.

Sam gave another shrug. 'It was just a suggestion.'

Like hell it was! He had come back in here spoiling for a fight. Well, the mood she was in—confusion mixed up with not a little uncertainty as to her own feelings towards this man—he was likely to get exactly that!

'I'll bear it in mind,' she said calmly.

'Of course you will.' Sam strode further into the

room, the coldness of his gaze raking over her assessingly. 'So, you're Crystal James,' he finally said speculatively.

So he had heard of her. So much for his earlier claim of having no idea what Molly was talking about—

'I went into the library and looked at the book Molly gave me last Christmas,' he explained. 'It's not a bad photograph of you on the back cover.'

'Thank you,' Crys accepted, every muscle in her body tensed defensively. Sam was now being just a little too pleasant, after the way he had strode out of here earlier. Just a little too amenable to be true... Besides, that challenging glint in his eyes was unmistakable.

'Hmm.' Sam nodded thoughtfully, his gaze still critically assessing. 'You're very young to have found such notoriety.'

'I believe you meant to say public popularity.'

'Did I?' he mused. 'Hmm, perhaps so. In either case, you're still very young.'

'Old enough to have got a university degree before going to Paris to study under the auspices of a master chef there. Old enough to work my passage through several London restaurants before opening up one of my own,' she claimed evenly. 'Old enough to have been married and widowed, too,' she added, aware that this was probably a below-the-belt shot, but deciding that Sam had asked for it; he was definitely being deliberately antagonistic.

'My, my—all that as well as television and book fame,' Sam drawled.

She drew in a deeply controlling breath; she would

not argue with him, no matter how much he tried to goad her into it, and that was that!

'I'm only the flavour of the month for the moment—excuse the pun! When I opened my restaurant the rest of it just seemed to follow. A case of just happening to be in the right place at the right time, I suppose.'

She was still slightly dazed herself at the speed with which she had shot to television stardom—was sure that she would never feel comfortable with the recognition that came her way even when she was doing something so mundane as her weekly shopping.

One minute she had been quietly—but successfully—running her restaurant in London; the next moment a producer, who happened to consider her restaurant his favourite, was offering her the chance to do a television series.

She had refused at first, had told him he had chosen the wrong person, that she was quite happy with her life the way that it was, thank you very much. But he refused to give up, and after months of badgering she had agreed to do one programme for him. The rest, as they say, had been history!

'Indeed,' Sam replied. 'I don't suppose your looks did you any harm, either.'

'I beg your pardon?' she gasped.

'I doubt any television producer would have been quite so interested in putting you on the small screen if you had been fat and forty!' he scorned.

He wasn't making this easy for her, she would give him that, Crys conceded as she bit the inside of her bottom lip to stop her sharp comeback. Fat and forty, indeed!

'I've never considered that the way I look has anything to do with my television success—'

'Then you're a fool!' Sam laughed mirthlessly. 'Because from where I'm standing it has everything to do with it!'

From where he—! He wouldn't be standing at all if he carried on the way he was going—Crys was going to very forcefully punch him on the nose! She might only be short, her build slight, but she was sure she could pack enough of a punch to rock this man back on his heels.

In fact, it would probably give her great satisfaction to do just that!

'I wouldn't advise it, if I were you,' Sam said.

'Sorry?'

'You will be if you even attempt to carry out the threat to hit me that I can see blazing in those candid grey eyes. You're quite a little virago when roused, aren't you?' he told her admiringly.

Add condescending to his list of faults, Crys thought furiously. 'Quite the little virago', huh!

'I would much rather see you aroused in another way,' he began huskily, suddenly much closer than Crys would have wished.

'Sam,' she said mildly, causing him to pause long enough to look at her enquiringly. 'Go to hell!' she told him forcefully, once she was sure she had his full attention.

To her surprise—or was it chagrin?—he began to laugh, a low husky laugh that completely transformed his austere expression into one of boyish charm. The last thing she wanted!

A remote, cynical Sam she could just about cope with; a Sam who had laughing green eyes and a boyish grin was a little harder to withstand. In fact she found she couldn't move as Sam lightly grasped the tops of her arms before planting a firm kiss onto her startled lips.

'What did you do that for?' she demanded indignantly as he straightened and released her.

He still grinned. 'For being you, I suppose: slightly naïve, extremely vulnerable—but very kissable!'

And she, it seemed, had no say in the matter! Damn cheek of the man. Just who did he think he was?

Molly's brother was who he was—the brother she so obviously adored. And Crys was a guest in his house. But that still didn't give him the right to kiss her whenever he felt like it!

'Don't do that again,' she bit out tautly.

'Or?' Sam prompted, that sculptured mouth still curved into a smile.

A smile she hardened herself to resist. 'Or,' she continued, 'I'd have no wish to upset Molly by explaining to her that I have to cut my visit short because her brother chooses to take advantage of the situation, but—'

'But you'll do so if you have to,' he finished scathingly. '"Take advantage of the situation"!' he repeated. 'What an old-fashioned expression!'

Crys met his gaze unflinchingly. 'I'm an old-fashioned type of woman.'

'Meaning?' His eyes narrowed speculatively.

'I'm sure you can work that out for yourself,' she retorted.

He gave a mocking inclination of his head, his gaze challenging. 'I'm sure I can.'

She was sure he could too. No matter what he might think, no matter what sort of women he usually associated with, she wanted him to know she was not a candidate for his next affair!

'Now, if you wouldn't mind, I would like to clear away and go to bed,' she told him pointedly.

'Alone?' he taunted softly.

'Definitely!' she snapped, the colour in her cheeks caused by anger rather than embarrassment at the subject of their conversation. 'Look, Sam, I don't think I can put this any more clearly than I already have—'

'No, you've been pretty—succinct so far,' he allowed.

'Then why do we still seem to have a problem?' she said exasperatedly.

'We don't,' he replied. 'If you can manage to keep your hands off me, I'm sure I can endeavour to do the same.'

'Of all the—'

'Yes?' Sam urged as she broke off incredulously.

'Never mind,' she muttered, turning away. 'For Molly's sake, I suggest we try to at least be polite to each other.'

'I think we've gone way past the polite stage, Crystal.' He refused her request. 'In fact, I'm not sure we ever reached it!'

She didn't think they had either. She felt as if she and Sam had jumped from being complete strangers to people who were far too intimate with each other, both conversationally and physically. Which, to Crys, in itself, considering this last year of emotional trauma, was incredible!

'Maybe not,' she said heavily. 'But I'm sure we can try to make some sort of effort now. If only in front of Molly,' she added firmly.

'I'm sure we can try,' he agreed. 'Whether or not we'll succeed is another matter!'

It wasn't going to be easy, Crys inwardly conceded, not when she was aware of Sam's every movement, reacted to every comment he made. As for Sam...! He just seemed to enjoy getting those reactions out of her—in one way or another!

'I'll take Merlin up with me, then.' Sam straightened, walking over to the kitchen door before pausing. 'Oh, and, Crystal...?'

She instantly tensed, meeting his gaze warily. 'Yes?'

His mouth twisted. 'You may, as you say, have acquired your television fame by being in the right place at the right time, but at the moment you're in my place and in my time—and if one iota of your success invades the privacy of my home—' his voice had hardened glacially '—you—and it!—will go straight out the front door. Is that clear?'

She raised her chin. 'As crystal,' she bit out.

He paused briefly. 'There's nothing in the least clear about you. You have more layers to you than— Oh, to hell with this!' He threw up his hands in defeat. 'I'm going to bed!'

And Crys was quite happy to let him go.

At least she could breathe again once he had gone, even if her legs were shaking so badly from the encounter that once again she had to lean back against one of the kitchen units.

She closed her eyes wearily. *She* was layered? Sam was so complex she didn't even know where his layers began!

She wished, and not for the first time, that she had

never come here—never met Sam, never— Well, just never met the man!

The next five days were going to be a definite trial for her—and she already knew that Sam, no matter what he had said just now, was not going to make them any easier for her!

CHAPTER TEN

'I APPRECIATE that she's one of your oldest friends, Molly. But that still doesn't tell me why you invited someone like her here!'

Crys had been on her way down the stairs when she'd first heard the sound of voices in the sitting room, realising as she did so that, despite it only being a little after eight o'clock in the morning, both Molly and Sam must have come down before her.

She had intended leaving brother and sister to talk, and was making her way quietly down the hallway towards the kitchen when she overheard Sam's last comment and came to an abrupt halt.

'Someone like her'? Could he possibly mean *her*? Crys wondered. It certainly sounded like it.

'She told me,' Sam said in reply to Molly's quieter response. 'And I know it can't have been easy for her. But, nevertheless, Crystal James is the last person you should have invited to my home, of all places!'

Crys's brow furrowed into a perplexed frown. Exactly what did he mean by that last remark?

She was aware of the fact that she was standing in the hallway, blatantly listening to a private conversation between Molly and her brother, but she couldn't have moved now if her life had depended on it—felt as if her feet were welded to the carpeted floor.

'Yes, that must have been awful for her too, so soon after her husband's death,' Sam conceded in answer to Molly's next comment. 'But the fact remains that—'

'You just don't want her here!' Molly's voice became audible in her anger.

'No, I don't,' Sam confirmed harshly. 'And you, of all people, should know why I don't,' he added vehemently.

Crys was totally stunned by that vehemence. Okay, so her relationship with Sam seemed to veer between the two opposites of hot and cold—but never, during those moods had she ever had the impression he actively disliked her...

'It's been ten years now, Sam.' Molly's voice was still loud enough to be heard. 'Isn't it time you moved on?'

'I have moved on, damn it!' he rasped. 'It's other people who haven't!'

'You don't know that—'

'And I'm not about to find out through your friend Crystal, either!' Sam stated angrily.

'Why do you call her that?' Molly asked.

'Crystal?' Sam repeated impatiently. 'Because to me Crys is a man's name.'

'And Crystal is totally feminine,' Molly conceded. 'Hmm,' she added thoughtfully.

'Exactly what does that mean?' Sam demanded irritably.

'Nothing,' Molly dismissed lightly. 'But you do like her, don't you?'

'What the hell does that have to do with anything?' he returned swiftly. 'Molly, you're deliberately missing the point—'

'Am I?' she came back just as quickly. 'I'm not so sure.'

'What does that mean?' Sam said angrily. 'Molly, I'm warning you. Don't start any sort of matchmaking between your friend and me! Crystal is a public figure; she owns and runs a restaurant in London. And I—'

'You're a reclusive hermit living in the wilds of Yorkshire,' Molly finished dryly. 'But it wasn't always that way, was it? Don't you miss any of that life, Sam? Don't you wish—?'

'No, I don't!' he came back. 'I don't miss a damn thing about that artificial life—not the people, not the places, nothing. Do I make myself clear?'

'As crystal—'

'Don't you start!' Sam retorted furiously.

'What did I say?' Molly sounded puzzled. 'Oh. Crystal,' she realised belatedly, her voice sounding amused now.

Yes. Crystal. She was still standing in the hallway, eavesdropping on a conversation she was sure Molly and Sam would rather wasn't overheard by anyone!

Move, she instructed herself. Move before one or both of them comes out of the sitting room and finds you standing here and knows you've been blatantly listening to their conversation.

'And another thing,' Sam continued accusingly, 'Crystal is under the misapprehension that I'm your brother!'

Crys had been about to continue quietly down the hallway to the kitchen, but Sam's words once again halted her in her tracks.

But Sam *was* Molly's brother—wasn't he…?

She didn't wait to hear Molly's reply, deciding that she had already heard enough. More than enough!

Merlin stood up as Crys entered the kichen, but she

was too shaken by what she had just overheard to care whether he felt friendly today or not, reaching out to scratch him absently behind one furry ear.

Incredibly, Sam's last comment seemed to imply that he *wasn't* Molly's brother. But if he wasn't her friend's brother, who was he?

Crys remembered she had called him Mr Barton when she'd first arrived, a name he'd seemed to take exception to, insisting she call him Sam instead. Could that possibly be because his name wasn't Barton, the same as Molly's, at all? But if his name wasn't Barton, then what was it...?

She poured herself a coffee from the percolator before sitting down at the kitchen table, more than a little taken aback by what she had just overheard.

Molly had always called Sam her brother—had talked about him incessantly when they were at school together, had obviously hero-worshipped him then.

As she obviously still did...

But was that in a sisterly way? Molly had mentioned something about it being ten years now... But ten years since what? Ten years ago Molly had appeared in the sixth form of Crys's boarding-school...

Crys shook her head. This was just too confusing. She didn't—

'Ah, here you are!' Molly said happily as she came into the kitchen, seemingly unaffected by her day of travelling yesterday, or the jet-lag she must be suffering, looking bright and beautiful in a sky-blue jumper and black denims. 'Sam and I were just wondering if you would be awake in time to accompany us on Merlin's walk.' She smiled warmly as she poured herself a coffee and sat down at the table with Crys.

Crys looked at her friend frowningly, knowing that up until a few minutes ago the two had been wondering nothing of the kind! But Molly certainly looked none the worse for her recent conversation with her brother—with Sam, she corrected awkwardly—whereas Crys always came away from conversations with Sam feeling as if she had been in the middle of a war zone!

Molly looked at her searchingly. 'Did you sleep okay?' she asked concernedly. 'Only you're looking a little pale,' she explained.

She felt thoroughly confused! She no longer had any idea what Molly's relationship was to Sam. Worse, Sam had told Molly quite categorically that he didn't want Crys here.

In the circumstances, she was fast coming to the conclusion that she didn't want to be here, either!

Ordinarily Crys would simply have asked Molly for an explanation concerning her relationship with Sam. Up until five years ago that was what she would have done. Even a year ago she might have done the same thing. But with yesterday's unfinished conversation about James already hanging between the two women Crys felt loath to bring up her confusion concerning Molly's connection to Sam!

'I slept fine, thanks,' she answered—it had only been in the last few minutes that she had started to feel totally disorientated. 'But would you mind if I gave the walk a miss this morning?' She smiled to lighten her refusal. 'I have a few telephone calls to make.' She pointedly held up her mobile telephone.

'Not business, Crys,' Molly protested predictably.

'You told me you weren't even going to think about work for a week!'

Crys gave a rueful smile. 'I can't help but think about it, Molly; you know that.'

Her friend sighed. 'I suppose so. But can't the calls wait until later?'

They could. But Crys needed to put a little time between herself and Molly and Sam, needed to be able to think clearly for a while. She might even go off for a walk on her own once the other two had left.

'No, I really need to call Gerry,' she said firmly, referring to the manager of her restaurant. 'Besides, it will give you and Sam a little time to yourselves,' she added brightly.

Her friend grimaced. 'A little of Sam goes a long way!'

Crys was already well aware of that! But, nevertheless, she had no intention of going out with the two of them this morning. She simply wouldn't know what to say to either of them at the moment. Besides, she felt uncomfortable being here at all after Sam had so determinedly stated his preference in that direction!

'You'll have a lovely time catching up on all your news,' Crys assured Molly; Sam might even tell Molly about the woman Caroline, who had telephoned him two days ago, just so that she knew he wasn't totally reclusive!

'I—'

'Are you two ready yet?' Sam barked as he strode forcefully into the kitchen, wearing denims and a black jumper today, his face freshly shaved.

'Good morning, Sam,' Crys greeted him pointedly;

he might not want her here, but good manners cost him nothing!

'Morning,' he returned grudgingly, green eyes dark with irritation.

Molly stood up reluctantly. 'I'll just go and change into my walking boots.'

'Make it quick,' Sam snapped.

Crys couldn't help looking at the two of them and searching for the likeness that would claim they were brother and sister, after all—despite what Sam might have said to the contrary.

But Molly's hair was red where Sam's was almost black, Molly's eyes brown where Sam's were green, and there was no similarity at all in their facial structure. And yet Crys remembered feeling a stirring of familiarity the first time she saw Sam's face clean-shaven. She had assumed it was because he must bear some resemblance to Molly. But he obviously didn't...

Who was he?

She shook her head, knowing she was unlikely to find the answer to that question unless Sam chose to tell her. Which she already knew he wouldn't do. He—

'What are you staring at?' he challenged.

Him! Without realising it Crys had continued to stare at Sam long after Molly had left the room in order to change her boots. Staring at him but not really seeing him as she became lost in thought.

'Sorry,' she muttered awkwardly as she turned away.

'Aren't you coming with us?' He frowned darkly at the realisation she hadn't moved to put on her own boots.

'I thought I would stay here. If that's okay with you?' she added belatedly, the thought suddenly occurring to her that he might not like leaving her alone in his home.

He shrugged into the thick jacket that had hung behind the kitchen door. 'Please yourself what you do,' he replied off-handedly.

Crys gave him a considering look. 'You really do dislike having people around you, don't you?' she said.

His gaze narrowed. 'What's that supposed to mean?'

She shook her head. 'Nothing,' she sighed. 'Is it okay with you if I stay here?' she pressed.

'I told you, please yourself,' he returned, that green gaze still watching her guardedly. 'Did you sleep okay? Only you're—'

'—looking a little pale,' she finished for him. 'So Molly's already told me.'

'Well?' he demanded.

'I slept fine,' she answered. 'I just— Can't you just accept that sometimes I prefer my own company to that of others too?' There was no doubt about it; she had definitely been rattled by the conversation she had overheard.

'And this happens to be one of those times?' He raised dark brows over mocking eyes. 'From what I've heard you spend too much time on your own as it is.'

Her cheeks flushed at the rebuke. 'Perhaps,' she conceded tightly, knowing she had been quite reclusive this last year. Or at least as reclusive as running a restaurant and recording television programmes would allow!

Sam warmed to his subject. 'Isn't that a little ungrateful of you on this occasion? After all, Molly has
come all the way here from New York just to see
you.'

'And you,' she batted back.

'And me,' he conceded. 'Are you sure there's nothing wrong, Crystal?' he asked, his gaze suddenly
sharp as an idea seemed to occur to him. 'Have you
been downstairs long?' he prompted suspiciously.

'Not long, no.' She stood up, walking over to the
sink to wash up her mug, deliberately avoiding looking at him.

But long enough!

Long enough to know how much this man didn't
want her here. Long enough to be thoroughly lost as to
his relationship to Molly. Or the woman Caroline—
let alone the times he had kissed her. Long enough
to know that she wanted to leave!

Sam lightly grasped her arm and swung her round
to face him, looking down intently into her face for
several long seconds. 'They do say eavesdroppers
never hear anything good about themselves.'

She raised her chin, flicking the silky hair back
over her shoulders as she did so. She could deny having overheard any of his conversation with Molly, but
to do so would be a blatant lie. She had an idea Sam
would know she was lying too.

'Is that what they say?' she replied. 'Personally, I
was taught it was rude to say anything about a person
behind their back that you wouldn't say to their face.'

'I was told that too,' he agreed. 'We weren't talking
about you, Crystal. Only—only the situation.'

'To my knowledge, that's the first time I've ever
been called a situation,' she said.

'Crystal—'

'I can hear Molly coming back down the stairs,' she interrupted firmly.

He looked as if he were about to say To hell with Molly, but then he brought himself back under control, drawing in a deep, controlling breath before abruptly releasing Crys's arm. 'We'll talk later, Crystal.'

Molly had wanted to talk to her 'tomorrow'. Sam wanted to talk to her 'later'. But she wasn't sure, the way things were, that she wanted to talk to either of them!

Perhaps that was being a little unfair to Molly. After all, her friend had done nothing wrong—had actively defended her earlier when Sam had been so adamant he didn't want her here. Crys just felt so weary she wanted nothing more than to go back to London and forget about this whole visit. And Sam!

'We *are* going to talk, Crystal,' Sam told her harshly now.

'Are we?' she dismissed, turning to smile at Molly as she came back into the room. 'I'll make something for lunch while the two of you are out,' she promised.

'Lovely!' Molly accepted eagerly, before turning to give Sam a mocking look. 'After all, Sam much prefers your cooking to mine,' she added mischievously.

Crys didn't look at Sam at all—could already guess that he wasn't pleased by Molly's teasing. One thing she knew for certain about Molly's relationship to Sam—her friend certainly wasn't in awe of his black moods.

'I'll see you both later,' Crys said.

'Have fun!' Molly called out as she went through the back door, Merlin following eagerly at her heels.

Crys turned to look at Sam with a cool control she wasn't sure she actually felt, blonde brows raised questioningly.

He stared back gloweringly for several long seconds, before turning to go. 'Don't work too hard,' he drawled over his shoulder.

'I'll try not to,' she retorted.

He gave a humourless smile as he walked to the door. 'I think I preferred your attitude when you thought I was a mass murderer!'

'What makes you think I've changed my mind?' Crys called after him.

He turned, a grin lightening his features. 'Because I very much doubt you would have kissed a man you believe to be a mass murderer in the way that you kissed me yesterday!' came his parting shot, and the door closed softly behind him as he left.

Trust Sam to have the last word, Crys silently fumed. But then, he probably always did, she conceded ruefully as she heard the engine of the Land Rover start up. The tension started to leave her as she realised, with Molly and Sam's departure, that now she had a couple of hours' respite from Sam's unique brand of teasing.

Because there was no doubt about it. Sam was correct when he claimed *she* had kissed *him* yesterday. Only Molly's unexpected arrival had stopped it from being more than a kiss. Then how would she have been able to face Sam this morning?

She gave a pained grimace just at the thought of it. It hadn't happened, so she wouldn't think about it. She would cook instead; that always calmed her, freed her mind of all worries as she concentrated on what she was doing. And she needed to be calm and free from worries at the moment!

A search of the store cupboards and the fridge provided the ingredients for a cheese and broccoli quiche to go with salad and jacket potatoes for lunch, and Crys happily engrossed herself with kneading the pastry mix. Then the telephone began to ring.

Crys listened to the rings. One, two, three, right the way up to twelve, when they ended. Only for the phone to ring again seconds later.

So it was either family or a close friend ringing Sam. Which was fine to know, but she doubted Sam would appreciate it if she were to actually answer his call.

In fact, she knew he wouldn't!

Except the first twelve rings, followed by the phone starting to ring again was repeated a second time, then a third, by which time Crys knew it had to be urgent for the caller to be so persistent. It was no good. She had to answer it—whether it incurred Sam's wrath or not!

She hastily washed her hands, managing to pick up the receiver just as the rings ended. Only for the process to start all over again, a fourth time. 'Hello?' she greeted tentatively.

'Sam…?' came back a female voice uncertainly.

Crys grimaced, sure her voice sounded nothing like Sam's. 'I'm afraid he's not here at the moment. Can I take a message?' Surely Sam couldn't be annoyed with her for just taking a telephone message for him? Yes, he could, she instantly answered herself. But it was too late to worry about that now; she had already answered the call.

'Is that you Molly?' The woman still sounded unsure.

'Er, no, it isn't Molly, either.' Crys sighed at the predicament she had got herself into. 'I—er—I'm just a friend. A family friend,' she added hastily, sure that Sam didn't think of her as a friend at all! 'Neither Sam or Molly are here at the moment.'

'I see,' the woman replied slowly, obviously not seeing at all. 'Well, this is Sally Grainger, Sam's agent. Could you ask him to telephone me immediately he gets back? Tell him—tell him that—'

'Perhaps you would be better waiting until Sam calls you back?' Crys put in quickly, sure that Sam wouldn't like her telling him anything about a call she should never have answered in the first place!

'Just tell him that David Strong has broken his leg,' the woman told her lightly. 'Which poses a bit of a problem, when the hero of *Bailey* doesn't normally walk around with his leg in plaster!'

Bailey…? Crys knew that television programme. She might not own a television, and she might have very little time for watching one, anyway, but she would have had to live in a cave these last five years not to have heard about the long-running series *Bailey*, featuring the detective of the same name, played by the actor David Strong. She knew, too, that it had topped the viewing charts with each new series since its conception.

But what could the popular television programme possibly have to do with Sam…?

'Tell Sam the director wants him to write some feasible explanation into the plot for Bailey to be thumping about on crutches with his leg in plaster,' Sally Grainger explained. 'They really think it's that easy!' she added disgustedly.

'I'll tell him,' Crys came back faintly.

'Thanks,' the other woman said. 'Ask Sam to call me as soon as he gets in, will you?' she asked again, before ringing off.

Crys slowly replaced her own receiver, knowing she was no longer just pale; she had gone white.

Wyngard!

Not Barton at all, Crys now realised. Because after her conversation with Sally Grainger Crys now knew that Sam's full name was Sam Wyngard, and he was the successful writer for the last five years of the television series *Bailey*. He was also the Oscar-winning screenwriter eleven years ago of the highly-acclaimed film *Race Against Time*.

And with the realisation of exactly who Sam was came the knowledge of exactly why he had chosen to bury himself away here for the last ten years...

CHAPTER ELEVEN

'Mmm, something smells mouthwatering,' Molly enthused a couple of hours later as she came into the kitchen from outside, her cheeks glowing after her long walk in the fresh air.

Crys gave her what she hoped was a natural smile. 'Lunch should be ready in twenty minutes or so. Where's Sam?' she enquired casually, very aware of the fact that he hadn't followed Molly into the house.

Molly glanced back outside even as she removed her scarf and gloves. 'He mumbled something about checking the oil in the Land Rover,' she explained. 'Is there anything I can do?' she offered as Crys began to lay the table for the three of them.

'You can finish this while I make the salad, if you like.' Crys turned away. 'Er—I'm afraid I have to go back to London later today; the restaurant is very heavily booked over the next three nights, and Gerry is short-staffed.' She managed to have her head inside the fridge, looking for the ingredients of the salad, when she made the announcement, not sure that she would actually be able to look convincing when she came out with the lie.

'Oh, no!' Molly's acute disappointment could clearly be heard in her voice.

Crys felt momentary guilt at her friend's reaction. But after what she had overheard this morning, and having taken that telephone call earlier, Crys just knew she couldn't stay on here any longer.

134

As it was, she was dreading having to tell Sam she had taken the call at all. She knew that he was intelligent enough to put two and two together and guess that she had come up with the truth about him. After that she doubted they would even get as far as eating the lunch she had prepared!

'Do you really have to go?' Molly complained. 'After all, I've only just got here!'

'I know. And I'm sorry. I really am.' And she was; it wasn't Molly that she was trying to avoid. 'I am sorry, Molly, but—' She broke off as the door opened and Sam walked in with his usual arrogance of movement.

Crys turned away, her embarrassment acute with the knowledge of who he was still fresh in her mind.

'Sorry about what?' he questioned as he looked at the two women suspiciously.

'Crys has to leave later today,' Molly told him disappointedly. 'I told you not to ring Gerry.' She turned to Crys.

Sam frowned darkly. 'Who's Gerry?'

'The manager of my restaurant,' Crys provided, avoiding looking at him by taking the quiche out of the Aga.

'Obviously not a very good one if he can't cope without you for a few days,' Sam observed scathingly.

Crys straightened, her face flushed from indignation as much as from the heat of the Aga. 'He happens to be an excellent manager,' she defended. 'But we're short-staffed, and the restaurant is busy—'

'So busy that you can't take a few days' holiday?' Sam interrupted disbelievingly.

Crys glared across the room at him, wondering why

he was bothering to protest at her leaving after what he had said this morning. 'As it happens—yes!' she snapped.

He shook his head. 'Sounds like an excuse to me,' he replied, helping himself to a tomato and biting into it as if it were an apple.

'Excuse?' Crys echoed tensely, still having trouble meeting his pentrating gaze.

'Molly assures me you're a workaholic, Crystal,' he said. 'But no one's indispensable, you know.'

Her mouth tightened. 'I have a responsibility—'

'You need a holiday,' he cut in, green gaze raking over her critically.

She might well do—but she certainly wasn't getting one staying here!

'I'll take one later in the year,' she dismissed. 'When I have more time.'

'Will you?' he said disbelievingly.

'Look—'

'Molly, would you mind going out and feeding Merlin for me?' Sam turned to smile at Molly even as he cut smoothly across Crys's continued protests. 'His food is outside in the shed,' he added helpfully.

'Sure,' Molly accepted lightly, moving to the door. 'But do me a favour while I'm gone, will you?' She paused, giving a rueful grin. 'Try and talk Crys out of leaving, hmm?'

'I thought that was what I was doing,' he murmured softly, once he and Crys were alone in the kitchen. 'What's going on, Crystal?' he prompted hardly.

She looked across at him. And then wished she hadn't as all the things she had read about him ten years ago came flooding back. Those ten years hadn't been kind to him, she noted, which was probably the reason he had seemed only vaguely familiar to her when she first met him. Photographs of him ten years ago had shown the laughingly handsome face of a man completely secure in his own invincibility. An invincibility that had since come crashing down around his ears...

'Nothing is going on.' She dismissed his query. 'I've already explained—'

'It's too convenient, Crystal.' He stood up forcefully, suddenly making the kitchen appear much smaller as he took a couple of steps towards her. 'Look, I know you don't like what you overheard me saying this morning,' he continued, 'but it was only from a personal view. Molly is going to be very upset if she finds out you're leaving because of that.'

And no matter what else had happened in this man's life, he did care about Molly. What he was to Molly Crys still hadn't been able to work out, but she accepted the affection was there; in the circumstances, she knew that no friend of Molly's would ever have been invited here if it weren't!

'She isn't going to find out.' Crys shook her head. 'Not from me, anyway.'

'Crys!' Sam reached out and grasped the tops of her arms, shaking her slightly. 'I'm trying to say—and not very successfully, it appears!—that I don't want you to leave on my account.'

She looked up at him searchingly. He was a hard man. An uncompromising man. But was he also a man who could be cruel enough to drive a woman into taking her own life?

Crys simply didn't know!

The man who had kissed her with such tenderness

and passion, perhaps not. But this other man, this hard, uncompromising one—she just didn't know!

'Answer me, damn it!'

She swallowed hard. 'I told you, the restaurant is busy—'

'And you're asking me to believe that feeble excuse for your leaving so suddenly?' Sam rasped.

'I'm not asking *you* to believe anything!' Crys returned heatedly. 'This may be your home, but Molly was the one who invited me here; if I owe an explanation to anyone, then it's to her. And she—'

'Doesn't believe you any more than I do,' he cut in. 'Does her friendship mean so little to you that you would hurt her by leaving in this abrupt way?'

'No, of course it doesn't,' she cried protestingly. 'But—'

'But what?' Sam challenged hardly. 'Is it because I've kissed you a couple of times? Is that what you find so unacceptable that you're going to leave? You didn't seem to mind at the time!'

The colour blossomed and then faded from her cheeks as the truth of his accusation hit her. No, she hadn't minded those kisses. And that was another reason she had to leave here. She needed space, and time, to decide exactly what those kisses had meant to her. Because they had meant something...

Her chin rose defensively. 'Don't try and make that into something it wasn't, Sam,' she told him. 'We're both adults, and have hardly never been kissed,' she continued. 'But that doesn't mean it was any more than a brief mutual attraction.'

'Doesn't it? *Doesn't it?*' he repeated, pulling her inexorably nearer, his gaze mere inches from her own now, their breath mingling warmly. 'Do I give the impression I go around just kissing women whenever I feel like it?'

Crys forced herself not to let her own gaze waver from meeting the intensity of his. 'I don't know—do you?'

'No, damn it, I don't! In fact, I can't remember when I last— But you—you just cry out to be kissed!'

'Sounds like an excuse to me.' She deliberately mocked his earlier comment to her, wondering about that unfinished sentence; he couldn't remember when he last—what? Kissed a woman? No, she couldn't believe that. After all, there was the woman Caroline in his life, at least. And Sally Grainger had behaved as if she knew him rather well too. Also, there was Molly...

'No excuse, Crystal,' Sam bit out gratingly. 'I make no apology for kissing you.'

She eyed him challengingly. 'Did I ask you to?'

'No, but—' He sighed. 'I do owe you an apology for what I said this morning about not wanting you here.'

'I shouldn't have been listening.' Her cheeks flushed fiery red as she recalled the earlier shock that had held her locked in place, making it impossible for her not to overhear his conversation with Molly.

'Will you let me finish this apology?' he cried impatiently. 'It may be the only one you'll ever hear from me.'

She already knew that he wasn't a man who backed down from statements made, and was surprised he was apologising at all.

'Go ahead. If it will make you feel better.'

'It's not intended to make me feel better—' He drew in a deeply controlling breath. 'Has anyone told you that you are an infuriating woman, Crystal Webber?'

Her mouth quirked. 'Not recently, no.'

'Well, you are.' He released her, turning away to thrust his hands into his denims pockets. 'Look, the fact is, Crystal, I don't want you to leave.'

'Sorry?' She wasn't sure she had heard him correctly. Surely he couldn't really have just said that he—

He turned sharply, glaring across the room at her. 'I said I don't want you to leave!' he bit out forcefully.

'Well, I think that makes it a majority vote of two against one,' Molly announced brightly as she came back into the house, bringing a gust of cold air and Merlin in with her. 'But I doubt you have to shout it so loudly, Sam, that they can hear you across two counties,' she added with an affectionate grin in his direction.

Sam glared back at her, before turning to encompass Crys in that same angry glance. 'Women!' he exclaimed disgustedly, before turning on his heel and striding from the room, slamming the door behind him.

'Men!' Molly countered with a knowing grimace. 'Dear, dear—what have you been doing to Sam, Crys?' she prompted interestedly.

She hadn't done anything to him! Except—except—if her instincts were correct—those kisses had meant more to Sam than just a mutual attraction, too...

Too...?

Yes, too.

No! She *couldn't* care about Sam! *Care* about him? It was more than that. Much more than that...!

'Hey, are you okay, Crys?' Molly came over concernedly. 'You've gone very pale.'

Pale? Pale! It was surprising she hadn't collapsed altogether with the realisation that had just hit her between the eyes with the force of a sledgehammer!

She had fallen in love with Sam Wyngard!

She gave a groan, moving to sit down—before she fell down. What had she done? *What had she done?*

'Crys?' Molly looked really worried now, coming down on her haunches beside Crys to take her cold hands within her much warmer ones. 'Crys, what is it?'

She shook her head, desperately fighting the dizziness that had come over her. 'Would you mind if I went to my room and lay down for a while? I—lunch is ready—'

'Never mind lunch,' her friend dismissed impatiently. 'Tell me what's wrong!'

Molly was her closest friend, had always been her staunchest ally, her confidante—but until Crys knew what Molly's relationship was to Sam her own feelings towards him weren't something she could possibly discuss with the other woman.

'I'm just tired, I think,' she excused awkwardly. 'I'm sure I'll be okay once I've rested for a while.'

She wasn't sure of any such thing—in fact, she wasn't sure she was ever going to be completely okay again!

'All right,' Molly agreed reluctantly as she straightened. 'But I really think you should reconsider going back to London this afternoon. I don't think you should even be thinking about returning to work just yet.'

She had even more reason for leaving this afternoon now! In fact, nothing would stop her getting as far away from here as quickly as possible!

'I'll be fine,' Crys reassured her as she stood up. 'And please make sure you and—and Sam eat the lunch I've prepared. You know how I hate waste,' she added on her way to the door.

'I'll come up and check on you later,' Molly called after her.

'Fine,' Crys agreed distractedly, more interested in not running into Sam on her way upstairs than she was in what Molly would do later.

She was lucky. Sam was nowhere in sight as she hurried up the stairs and along the hallway to her bedroom, slightly breathless from her flight after closing the door behind her.

Tears fell hotly down her cheeks. James! Oh, James! How could she possibly have fallen in love with a man so unlike him? With a man she wasn't even sure James would have liked, let alone approved of? But the two men had met, hadn't they, when James came here to design the interior of the house? Had they liked each other? Crys wondered.

But what did it matter if the two men had liked each other or not? It appeared that she was capable of falling in love with both of them!

She didn't want to fall in love. Didn't want to love anyone—least of all a man like Sam Wyngard.

What sort of man was he really? The man she knew now, despite his hard exterior, had proved himself to be compassionate and caring, even if he did try to hide those qualities behind a barrier of arrogance.

All she knew of the Sam from ten years ago was what she had read in the newspapers at the time. It hadn't made pleasant reading, she admitted, but how much of what she had read was the truth? People didn't change, not really. So if Sam was compassionate and caring now, surely he must have been so then, too?

What was the point of all this soul-searching? she admonished herself. Sam was a man beyond any woman's reach, let alone for a permanent relationship, that much she had learnt about him. And anything else would be completely unacceptable to her, so—

She lost her balance and was shot forcefully across the room as the door was suddenly thrust open behind her, turning dazedly to find Sam standing in the doorway.

'What's wrong with you?' he demanded without preamble.

'Well, at the moment I'm trying to pick myself up off the floor.' She exaggerated the effect of being knocked across the room by his sudden entrance, finding it hard to look at him at all with the knowledge of her love for him fresh in her mind.

'Don't prevaricate, Crystal,' he countered, coming further into the room and closing the door behind him. 'Molly says you aren't well.'

'Molly is exaggerating—'

'Molly no doubt has her faults, but that isn't one of them. So what's wrong, Crystal?' he demanded again, arrogantly.

She stared at him wordlessly, knew she couldn't have spoken even if she had tried. Besides—what could she possibly say? Against all her instincts, against all sense, she had fallen in love with this man.

And she wasn't sure the pain of it wasn't going to kill her...

Sam crossed the room in two easy strides, gently clasping her arms to look searchingly into her face, a deep frown between those dark green eyes as his gaze held her mesmerised.

'It would never work between us,' he said quietly.

'No,' she acknowledged huskily.

'It would be pure madness on both our parts to ever imagine that it would,' he continued gently.

'Yes.'

'You live in London, and I have no intention of ever leaving Yorkshire.'

'Yes.'

'You're everything I've tried to avoid in a woman the last ten years.'

Remembering what little she knew of the events of ten years ago, she could imagine that she was!

'Yes,' she said again.

His hands tightened. 'Then what the hell am I doing in here?'

Crys swallowed hard. 'I don't know.'

'Yes, you do,' he instantly rebuked her.

'No, I—'

Yes, she did! She knew that Sam was as powerless as herself to fight the attraction between them. Even though he obviously wanted to!

She shook her head. 'I was very much in love with my husband.' Was? When had it become the past tense...?

'Yes,' Sam grated.

'I'm not interested in another relationship,' she added firmly.

'No.'

She drew in a ragged breath. 'Tell me, when James was here working for you, did the two of you—?'

'Go out on drinking binges together? Confide in each other?' Sam finished scornfully. 'No. The former I don't believe either of us was interested in. And men don't actually do the latter too often. But did we like each other? Yes, I believe we did,' he murmured softly. 'Your husband was a very likeable man, Crystal.'

Her vision blurred with unshed tears. 'Yes, he was.' But Sam certainly was not; he had too many prickles to ever be called that!

His mouth twisted as he seemed to read her thoughts. 'Believe it or not, I never have a problem getting on with other men!'

Probably because he didn't treat other men as if they were the enemy—which he seemed to think women were! Well...most women. Molly certainly didn't come under that heading.

'I believe you,' she said. 'But what have either of us proved by this conversation?'

'That attraction to another person doesn't take into account the reasons why it shouldn't happen?' Sam replied.

Yes, they had more than proved that. But where did they go from here? Nowhere, came the resounding answer!

There was nowhere for them to go. No promise of a blossoming relationship. No light-hearted banter as they got to know each other better. No quiet dinners together. No trips to the theatre. No walks in the beauty of a bluebell wood. No quiet moments when they just enjoyed each other's company. There was just nowhere for a relationship between the two of them to go!

She straightened. 'I really do have to leave, Sam,' she told him firmly.

His answer was to bend his head slightly, his lips taking gentle possession of hers, heated desire instantly engulfing both of them as the kiss deepened.

Madness. Utter, complete madness. And yet at that moment Crys didn't doubt that it consumed both of them...

Her arms moved up about his shoulders, the soft curves of her body contoured perfectly against the hard muscles of Sam's chest and thighs, their lips so enmeshed it was as if they were one person.

Crys gave a slight sob in her throat as Sam's hands restlessly caressed the curve of her spine, the dip of her waist, the soft pout of her breasts. Her nipple rose to the sensuous touch of his fingertips, heat coursing through her body to nestle fluidly between her thighs.

She wanted him. Oh, how she wanted him—all of him—pressed so tightly against her nakedness that not even a breath of air separated them, wanted to know his full possession, to feel him deep inside her as—

Sam's mouth left her suddenly as he raised his head to turn and glare at the closed door. 'Damn!' he muttered frustratedly, his arms momentarily tightening about Crys's slenderness.

'What—?' Crys looked up at him dazedly, grey eyes mistily dark with desire.

'Sam...?' A knock sounded on the door to accompany Molly's tentative query.

A knock and a query that Sam had obviously heard the first time!

Crys pulled awkwardly out of his arms, desperately avoiding looking at Sam as she did so. The heated colour in her cheeks had paled to an ashen white, and she clasped her hands tightly together in front of her so that Sam shouldn't see their shaking.

'Crystal—?'

'I think you should see what Molly wants,' she cut in huskily, still avoiding his searching gaze.

'I'm not interested in what Molly wants—'

'Then perhaps you should be.' Crys looked at him now, her face deliberately expressionless.

He looked furious, both at the interruption and at Crys's response to it, a nerve pulsing in his tightly clenched jaw. 'Okay, I'll see what Molly wants,' he finally conceded. 'But then you and I have to talk.'

She shook her head. 'We've already talked. And the last few minutes changes nothing,' she added firmly as he would have spoken.

His mouth thinned. 'We'll see about that,' he muttered, before striding over to the door and wrenching it open. 'Yes, Molly?' His barely repressed violence was obvious in his tone.

Molly took an involuntary step backwards. 'I wouldn't have disturbed you…' She looked past Sam to give Crys a self-conscious grimace. 'Only you obviously couldn't hear the telephone up here with the door closed, and so—'

'Just spit it out, Molly,' Sam snapped impatiently. 'Whatever it is!'

She grimaced. 'Sally Grainger is on the telephone. She says it's urgent that she speak to you— What is it?' Molly glanced past Sam to look concernedly at Crys as she gave an involuntary gasp of dismay.

What it was was that Crys had just realised she had

completely forgotten—with what had happened since Molly and Sam returned from their walk—to give Sam the message concerning his agent's telephone call! And it was too much to hope Sally Grainger wouldn't mention that first call...

She turned reluctantly to look at Sam. 'I—I forgot to tell you. I—she called earlier,' she admitted. 'Sally Grainger, I mean,' she added lamely.

A shutter came down over those luminous green eyes and Sam's expression became a cold mask. 'And when she called earlier did she happen to say what she wanted?' Even his voice was softly cold and unemotional.

Crys swallowed hard, another quick glance at Sam telling her that she would get no help from him with her obvious discomfort. 'Some problem to do with the *Bailey* series, I think,' she revealed reluctantly.

She didn't think, at all—she had been told exactly what his agent's problem was! As she obviously now knew exactly who Sam was, too!

'I see,' Sam murmured icily, before turning sharply on his heel and walking towards the open doorway.

'Sam!' Crys cried out to him instinctively, knowing she couldn't just let him walk away from her like this. Although she had no idea what she could possibly say to stop him!

He paused, turning slowly to look at her. If anything his expression was even more forbidding than it had been a few moments ago. 'Yes?'

Yes, what? What could she possibly say to him that was going to make any difference? All the reasons they had given each other such a short time ago for why a relationship between them could never work still existed, and now there was one more. Sam knew that she knew exactly who he was!

'Nothing.' She sighed. 'Absolutely nothing,' she added heavily, wishing that both he and Molly would just go now and leave her to her own misery.

Sam gave an abrupt inclination of his head before turning to stride forcefully from the room, pausing only long enough to touch one of Molly's cheeks in acknowledgement then going downstairs to take his telephone call.

The silence between Crys and Molly, after Sam's abrupt departure, was as full of unasked questions—from both women—as it was unanswered questions.

CHAPTER TWELVE

AND those same questions remained unasked and unanswered for at least the first hour of the drive back to London.

Molly had decided to accompany Crys back to town and stay with her there for a few days rather than remain in Yorkshire with Sam. 'After all, it was you I came to see,' Molly had protested when Crys had expressed surprise at her friend's decision.

So the hours of solitude Crys had been looking forward to on her drive back to London hadn't materialised—although neither woman seemed inclined to break the silence between them. Crys because she simply had no idea what to say. Molly—well, after years of believing that Molly was an open book, Crys had to admit she had absolutely no idea what Molly was thinking!

'It wasn't Sam's fault, you know.'

Crys gave a nervous start as Molly broke the silence, glancing briefly at her friend before answering. 'Sorry?' She frowned her puzzlement.

What wasn't Sam's fault? That she had no idea of the true relationship between him and Molly? That he was completely unfathomable? That he had been so furiously angry when he'd returned from talking to Sally Grainger on the telephone?

Actually, 'angry' didn't quite describe his behavior when he'd joined the two women in the sitting room after taking his call; rude, arrogant and cold probably better described it—but most of all cold!

'Well, if you're going, don't you think you had better get on with it?' he had snapped at her insultingly, eyes as cold as the emeralds they so resembled.

'Sam!' Molly protested awkwardly. 'You're being incredibly rude,' she added as he made no response.

Sam didn't even spare Molly a glance, continuing to look down coldly at Crys as she sat in one of the armchairs. 'Fine,' he barked. 'It was nice meeting you, Ms James.' He nodded with freezing dismissal. 'I hope you have a safe journey home,' he concluded, before turning challengingly to Molly. 'Polite enough for you?' he bit out scathingly.

She winced self-consciously. 'Yes. But—'

'Leave it, Molly,' Crys advised wearily, knowing that, the mood Sam was in, conversation of any kind was only going to make the situation worse.

'Yes, leave it, Molly.' Sam echoed her words scornfully. 'Ms James and I have said all that we need to say to each other.' He strode from the room without a second glance for either woman.

And that was the last Crys, at least, had seen of him...

Molly, it appeared, had gone to say her goodbyes to him, informing Crys when she returned of her decision to return to London with her.

To say Crys had been surprised by her friend's decision would be an understatement. Molly had only just arrived in Yorkshire and must surely want to spend some time with Sam...?

'Rachel,' Molly bit out curtly now, in answer to Crys's puzzled query. 'Rachel Gibson,' she enlarged pointedly as Crys continued to look blank.

That was what Molly was claiming wasn't Sam's fault!

Rachel Gibson. Beautiful, talented actress. Fiancée of the award-winning screenwriter Sam Wyngard. She had taken an overdose of sleeping tablets after Sam had broken off their engagement amid accusations he was having an affair with another woman.

Although that other woman obviously played no part in the solitary life he now led…

Or did she? Crys wondered now, with a sideways glance at Molly. Admittedly Molly would only have been sixteen ten years ago, when all of this took place, but—

'Sam didn't realise it when he met her, but Rachel was unbalanced,' Molly continued quietly. 'Oh, not noticeably so,' she conceded. 'Only where Sam was concerned, it seemed. Once they became engaged she believed every woman he met, every woman who ever came near him, wanted him. Her jealous rages became embarrassingly unbearable for Sam, so much so that eventually the only way out that he could see was to end their engagement.'

At which point, presumably, Rachel Gibson had taken the overdose…

As Crys recalled, the newspapers at the time had told a different story—one of Sam's deliberate cruelty to Rachel by walking out on her several times in public, of her humiliation at his publicised relationships with other women, of days, weeks, when she didn't even see her fiancé, of her final heartbreak when he ended their engagement and walked out of her life for ever.

A lot of women might have been relieved to be free of such a monster, but Rachel Gibson, once recovered, had sobbed out her love for Sam in one of the daily newspapers.

Crys had had several hours this morning, as she'd waited for Molly and Sam's return from their walk, to remember all that she could about that time ten years ago. One particular newspaper had been full of the story for weeks: from Rachel's attempted suicide through to her slow recovery when she claimed to still be in love with Sam and to want him back in her life. So it wasn't too difficult to remember most of the very personal details of their broken engagement.

But as far as Crys recalled there had been no reference to Rachel as the jealously possessive woman that Molly was now describing to her...

'I'm sure it was a very difficult time for him,' Crys returned non-committally.

'Difficult' didn't quite describe the public and private reaction to Sam Wyngard after Rachel had taken the overdose. Overnight, it seemed, he had been ostracised by the public and his peers alike: a play he had written, that was being performed in the West End at that time, had closed down only two weeks after Rachel's attempted suicide, due to lack of attendance, the Oscar nomination he had received for his screenplay of *Dark Knight* had been embarrassingly unsuccessful, and a new series of his that had been halfway through filming had been suddenly dropped by the television company. In only a matter of weeks the name Sam Wyngard had become a dirty word, the man's career had been in tatters—probably his private life too.

Which, presumably, was the reason he now lived like a hermit in the wilds of Yorkshire, his home appearing derelict from the outside as a deterrent to any-

one and everyone, his only companion a protective
Irish Wolfhound.

Although…

'He seems to have a success in the *Bailey* series,'
she said hopefully. Though she knew Sam Wyngard
never appeared at any of the award ceremonies where
his series usually swept the board.

'You don't believe a word I've said, do you?'
Molly sighed heavily at her side.

She frowned. 'Molly, it isn't for me to—'

'Pull over into this service station,' Molly cut in
firmly, pointing to the turn-off point that was fast
looming. 'I want your full attention while I talk to
you,' she added decisively.

Crys had no idea what Molly thought any of this
had to do with her, but she took the turn-off anyway,
driving into a parking space and turning off the engine before turning to look at her friend.

What she had been about to say got stuck in her
throat as she saw that Molly's expressive brown eyes
were swimming with unshed tears.

'Molly!' Crys reached out to hug her friend before
looking at her concernedly. 'If it's that important that
I believe you—'

'Of course it's important to me,' Molly choked, the
tears falling down her cheeks unchecked now. 'Sam
is—special. He's good, and kind, and generous, and
caring, and—'

'Okay, okay, I give up.' Crys held her hands up in
mock surrender, trying to coax a smile from her friend
with her own teasingly affectionate one. 'If you think
he's special then I'm sure that he is,' she placated
gently.

Molly brushed the tears away impatiently. 'If I

didn't know you better, Crys, I would say you're patronising me—'

'No, I'm not doing that,' she instantly assured her friend. 'Your perception of Sam is uniquely your own.' Even if the rest of the world totally disagreed with that perception…!

Molly smiled humourlessly. 'The world of acting, as I've learnt for myself these last few years, is extremely fickle. One minute you can be the darling, the centre of success, and the next you can be returned to obscurity, or as good as.' She gave a rueful shake of her head. 'But because of Sam's experience ten years ago I've kept my feet very much on the ground where my career is concerned, and I treat all the good things that have happened in my career so far with a certain amount of cynicism, taking care to maintain a private life for myself that is totally removed from it all. Which is why our friendship is so important to me,' she added emotionally. 'Oh, I know you have your own career, and the success that goes with it, but you don't allow any of that to impinge on your private life. Besides, our friendship existed long before either of us achieved the success we now have.'

'And it will continue to exist,' Crys assured her warmly. 'We've been through too much together to ever let anything destroy that.' Except… She was still unsure of how Molly had felt about James. And she still had no idea how Molly felt towards Sam, either. Besides a large dose of hero-worship, that was!

Molly reached out and clasped her hand. 'I—I don't— I've always felt so guilty about James!' she finally managed to burst out, her expression pleading now.

Crys stiffened, still not sure she felt up to some

last-minute confession of Molly's love for her own husband. But James, sadly, was dead, and she and Molly were still both very much alive. Surely if Molly had had the strength of character to allow Crys her happiness with James she now had compassion enough to accept how Molly had felt towards him?

'If I had just never introduced the two of you…'

If. Life, it seemed, was made up of ifs. If she and James had never met they would never have fallen in love. If they hadn't fallen in love then they wouldn't have married and found such happiness together. If James hadn't developed cancer then he would still be here with her now. If. If. If!

Everyone had ifs in their lives. Molly. She did. And Crys was sure that Sam must have a few ifs of his own, too!

'You're the closest thing to a sister I've ever had,' Molly continued. 'To know that it was my fault you met James, only to lose him again in that way…' She sighed shakily. 'You don't know how many times I've regretted introducing the two of you, unwittingly being the cause of so much pain to you—'

'The pain only came after he died, Molly,' Crys cut in protestingly. Another explanation for Molly's regrets concerning James suddenly seemed a possibility—not Molly's own love for him, but guilt at having been the reason the two of them had met at all, at Crys's ultimate loss of the man she loved. 'I had six wonderful months with James. Six months that I might otherwise never have had if it hadn't been for you. I don't regret a single moment of our time together. Not a single moment,' she added firmly as Molly looked ready to protest again.

Molly looked at her searchingly. 'You really mean that, don't you?' she said wonderingly.

'Of course I mean it,' Crys replied unhesitatingly, knowing she wouldn't have given up a moment of the time she'd had with James. Even if she had known of his illness before she'd met and fallen in love with him, she knew she would still have fallen in love with him...

Molly breathed shakily. 'After seeing your total distress at the funeral I— For months I put off seeing you, avoided any suggestion that the two of us meet, claimed work commitments that didn't exist,' she admitted.

Crys gave her friend's arm an affectionate squeeze. 'That was silly. And completely unnecessary.'

Molly gave her a doleful look. 'I must say you do seem much better than when I last spoke to you on the telephone...'

'I am better,' Crys assured her, realising that she actually was.

The heavy weight of sorrow that she had carried for the last year, first for her husband and then for her parents, seemed to have lifted. She was actually looking forward to returning to London. To talking to the customers in her restaurant. She was even looking forward to starting work on her new television series!

She gave a smile. 'It must be all that bracing Yorkshire air!'

Molly gave her a teasing look. 'Does that mean that meeting Sam had nothing to do with the change I sense in you?'

Crys frowned. Sam? What on earth could he have to do with the fact that life no longer looked quite so bleak and unlivable? After telling her earlier, twice, that they had to talk, the man hadn't even bothered to come out to the car and say goodbye to her before she left!

According to Molly he had wished them both a safe journey before going off for another walk with Merlin.

'Sam?' she repeated with a shake of her head. 'I have no idea what you're talking about, Molly,' she confessed, not even wanting to think at the moment about her emotions towards Sam Wyngard. She would have plenty of time to reflect on those once she was back in London...

'Rachel ruined his life ten years ago,' Molly said fiercely. 'In fact, she did a pretty good job of messing up all our lives for a time!'

Crys frowned uncertainly. 'She did?'

Molly nodded. 'Why do you think I had to change schools at sixteen? It was because Rachel ran to that newspaper with a pack of lies about Sam and blew up such a storm for the whole family that my parents decided it would be better to place me somewhere it wasn't public knowledge that Sam Wyngard was my brother,' she explained grimly.

'So your name isn't Barton...?' Crys was having difficulty keeping up with this conversation; Sam had clearly stated this morning that he *wasn't* Molly's brother!

'Of course it is.' Molly gave her a quizzical glance. 'Sam's father married my mother when I was twelve.'

Making Sam Molly's *stepbrother*! Why hadn't she thought of that before? Crys admonished herself self-disgustedly. Extended families and step-relations were all too common nowadays.

'But that isn't important now,' Molly went on. 'The

point is, I'm not about to let Rachel's lies ruin Sam's life for a second time!'

Crys leant back in her own seat, her expression wary now. 'What on earth do you mean?'

'Surely it's obvious why I wanted you to meet me in Yorkshire rather than London?' Molly said exasperatedly. 'You can't be so—so unaware of other men since James died that you didn't even notice how absolutely gorgeous Sam is?'

Of course she had noticed. Once she'd got past the scruffy hermit pose. He was so mesmerisingly attractive it would have been difficult not to. But that didn't mean—didn't mean—

'Molly,' she said slowly, 'this guilt you felt over my loss of James—you—I—you didn't deliberately delay your arrival in Yorkshire, did you? You didn't give Sam and I a couple of days on our own to get to know each other?' She frowned as the idea occurred to her. 'You didn't have some idea of trying to give me Sam as some sort of a replacement for James, did you?' She shook her head disbelievingly.

The idea seemed incredible, absolutely ludicrous, but—

'That would be very silly on my part, now, wouldn't it?' Molly said. 'I would need Sam's cooperation for that—and I'm sure you know him well enough after the last couple of days spent alone in his company to realise Sam won't be pushed into anything. By anyone.'

Crys still frowned, not exactly reassured by her friend's answer. It was noticeable—to her, at least—that Molly hadn't answered the first part of her question...

Of course she was relieved that Molly hadn't been

in love with James after all, but that knowledge didn't preclude Molly doing a bit of matchmaking in another quarter…

She drew in a deep breath. 'Yes, but—'

'But I'm not going to say I wouldn't have been overjoyed if my best friend and my brother had found themselves attracted to each other,' Molly interrupted. 'And I must also say there were a couple of occasions, after I arrived yesterday, when the two of you seemed to like each other very much!' She looked speculatively at Crys.

There was no way she could prevent the heated colour that flooded her cheeks. She knew that Molly couldn't have helped but be aware, on those couple of occasions, of the closeness between Sam and herself; the two of them had obviously been in each other's arms several times before Molly had interrupted them! Including earlier, when Molly had found Sam in her bedroom!

'There was a—a certain physical attraction,' she conceded impatiently. 'But for heaven's sake don't read anything more into it than that, Molly. I live in London. Run a restaurant. Have my own television programme—'

'Don't tell me that with all of that going on you don't have time for a man in your life?' Molly insisted. 'Because you were doing all those things when you were married to James.'

'I wasn't about to say that,' Crys denied. 'I'm merely pointing out the impracticality of there ever being more than that attraction between Sam and myself.' As Sam had done so succinctly earlier! 'We— our lives—are completely incompatible.'

'But—'

'End of subject, Molly,' she cut in, the steadiness of her gaze on Molly's a definite warning.

Her friend grimaced. 'Sam wants me to telephone him when we get back to London.'

'So?' Crys prompted warily; surely it was only natural for him to want to know they had arrived safely. Brotherly. *Stepbrotherly!*

In retrospect, Crys felt a little silly over the mistake she had made concerning Molly's possible relationship to Sam. But thankfully neither of them had realised where her over-active imagination had taken her this time!

But there was still this woman Caroline somewhere in Sam's life… Did Molly know about her? Crys simply had no idea—although, from what Molly had said, she very much doubted it.

'He asked me to let him know that you're okay—'

'Why shouldn't I be okay?' Crys exclaimed angrily.

Molly looked startled. 'He didn't say. Only that I was to call him when we got to London.'

Crys was furious at Sam's high-handedness in asking Molly to do any such thing. 'Just because the man has kissed me a couple of times, that doesn't give him the right—'

'Aha!' Molly pounced, eyes gleaming now.

'Aha, nothing!' Crys bit back, moving to switch on the ignition. 'This conversation is very definitely at an end, Molly,' she said firmly.

'Okay,' Molly accepted lightly.

Crys turned to give her friend a frowning glance before she had to give her attention to manoeuvring the car back onto the motorway. 'Methinks you're protesting too little,' she murmured with slow dissatisfaction.

'What a terrible misquote!' Her friend laughed softly, settling herself back in her seat and closing her eyes. 'I think I'll just have a little doze, if you don't mind; jet-lag seems to have caught up with me again.'

Conveniently so, as far as Crys was concerned. Oh, not that she doubted Molly was genuinely feeling the effects of the time-change between England and New York—it was just that she knew Molly wasn't averse to using it as an excuse not to have to continue with this conversation if she felt so inclined.

Nor to listen to any more of Crys's protests against there being any sort of relationship between herself and Sam!

Which there wasn't!

Was there…?

CHAPTER THIRTEEN

'I'M SORRY, Crys,' Gerry, the manager of her restaurant, came back from taking a telephone call. 'But the number for the birthday party this evening has changed again; we have one extra, making a total of twenty-five now.'

Crys looked up from the huge display of fruit she had been arranging. 'Great—an odd number. I'm beginning to wish I had never taken the booking. The only way I could take it at all was to book them in at nine-thirty, after I've fed all the other diners.' She stopped to ponder. 'I wouldn't have taken the booking at all if this Mr Gardener's secretary hadn't been so charming.'

'Male or female?' Gerry teased.

'Female,' Crys returned snippily.

'Then obviously this Mr Gardener is a man with good taste in restaurants and food.' Gerry grinned.

Crys gave a reluctant smile at his attempt at flattery. 'I only hope he appreciates all the extra work he's causing us by changing the number every couple of days,' she said. It had started out as eighteen people, but over the last three weeks, since the booking was first made, that number had slowly increased by seven.

Crys moved on from the fruit to arrange the flowers for the centre of the huge table that was taking over one half of her restaurant for part of the evening. But it was necessary to seat that many people together.

'Just add it to his bill.' Gerry shrugged. He was a short, sparely built man of forty. 'If he can afford to bring twenty-five people here to dinner for his own birthday then he isn't going to notice the inconvenience charge!'

'There's a hard streak in you, Gerry Smythe.' Crys laughed softly. 'And I couldn't possibly do that. I've already quoted a price per head to his secretary. With champagne and other drinks on top, of course.'

'Of course,' Gerry agreed, checking his watch. 'Still four hours until our first booking for the evening; is it okay if I pop home for a couple of hours and help Pam put the horrors to bed?'

'The horrors' were Gerry and Pam's six-year-old twin girls—and their father adored them both to distraction!

'Of course,' Crys instantly agreed. 'Everything here is pretty much under control, anyway. I just have to prepare another rainbow trout for guest number twenty-five before having a sit-down myself with my feet up for an hour.' She had been standing constantly for the last three hours as they readied the restaurant for this evening.

'I'll lay another place at the table before I go,' Gerry confirmed. 'Back by seven-thirty,' he promised on his way out.

'Thanks.' Crys gave him a distracted wave as she continued to arrange the flowers in a vase—yellow roses that had been especially requested for the party of twenty-four—no, twenty-five.

The last few weeks had been extremely busy ones

for her, and with the filming for her television programme starting next week she knew it wasn't going
to get any less busy.

But she was revelling in it, was enjoying her work
now in a way she hadn't done in months.

Wallowing in it might be a better description, came
a little voice inside her head.

That voice again! The stupid thing didn't seem to
want to go away just lately, and kept putting unlikely
thoughts into her head at the most ridiculous of times.

Thoughts like perhaps bumping accidentally into
Sam Wyngard...

How on earth she imagined she would ever do that
she had no idea, when he was buried in the wilds of
Yorkshire and she was back in the thick of things here
in London!

But she found herself thinking about him constantly. She would catch a glimpse of a man in the
street, or in a shop, who bore a slight resemblance to
him—tall and dark-haired—and for a brief moment
would mistakenly think it might be him. Because a
part of her ached to see Sam again...!

The part of her that was in love with him.

Which was all of her!

The feelings she had realised she had towards Sam
while staying in Yorkshire hadn't faded during the
four weeks since she'd returned to London. If anything they had intensified. Which was the reason that
little voice was taunting her about wallowing.

Molly had kept her promise that day four weeks
ago, and had telephoned Sam once they were back at
Crys's apartment. But he hadn't asked to speak to

Crys, and apart from the brief conversation he had had with Molly Crys had heard nothing from him since her return to London.

Not that she had expected to. Not really. Although she couldn't deny it would have been wonderful if she had. Quite what they would have said to each other she didn't know, but that didn't make the ache just to hear his voice any less.

As a consequence she had deliberately kept herself busy during the last weeks—had resumed a social life of her own while continuing to be a presence at the restaurant, plus put the finishing touches to the book that would be published to accompany this latest television series.

But, if she were honest, none of those things had made the slightest difference to the ache she felt inside her just for sound or sight of Sam!

She could have had no idea how totally unprepared she would be when that did finally happen!

'Another bottle of the same champagne on table three,' Gerry instructed the wine waiter efficiently as he came smoothly into the kitchen. 'The first of the Gardener guests have started to arrive,' he told Crys economically, while keeping a managerial eye on the staff as they bustled about the kitchen. 'Two of the peripheral guests, at a guess, not the guest of honour himself.'

'Fine.' Crys nodded, removing her apron before checking that her hair was still in the neat chignon she wore when cooking.

'You look great,' Gerry assured her warmly. 'As always.'

She gave him a grateful smile before hurrying out to the restaurant to personally welcome the first of the guests in the birthday party, and staying out front as the rest arrived in a steady stream after that.

Except for the final five, she noted with a frown when she realised it was almost ten o'clock. The guest of honour had not arrived yet, either. Although his guests were quite happily enjoying the vintage champagne he'd ordered to be served throughout the evening!

Well, it wasn't April the first, so this couldn't be an April Fool's joke, she decided after another frowning glance at her wristwatch. But even so—

'Crys!'

Her eyes widened in recognition of that voice even as she turned towards the door, her arms opening instinctively as a happily glowing Molly launched herself into them.

'I suppose it's too much to hope that I might receive the same enthusiastic greeting,' drawled an all too familiar voice.

Crys instantly stiffened, feeling her face pale as she slowly straightened away from a grinning Molly to steel herself for the confrontation ahead...

With Sam, looking lethally attractive in black dinner suit and snowy-white shirt!

Crys blinked as she took in his appearance: smilingly clean-shaven, with even his hair considerably shorter than when Crys had last seen him. Although the wariness in those dark green eyes was still there...

'Well?' He held his arms open invitingly, one dark brow quirked challengingly.

She couldn't look away from that compelling green gaze, and moved forward as if hypnotised—although at the last moment she did manage to clasp the tops of his arms, and so prevent them moving about the slenderness of her waist, before standing on tiptoe and kissing him on the cheek. A cheek that smelt achingly of the aftershave he'd worn in Yorkshire...!

Sam looked down at her with laughing green eyes. 'Is that it?' he asked.

'Of course,' Crys coolly replied, giving herself an inward shake as she forced herself to look away from him and smile questioningly at Molly, heated colour in her cheeks now. 'Why didn't you telephone and let me know that you wanted a table this evening?'

'But I did, me darlin',' Molly answered in the Irish brogue that was instantly recognisable—to an astounded Crys!—as that of the 'secretary' to Mr Gardener who had taken care of the details for this evening's booking.

'*You're* Mr Gardener?' Crys realised, totally puzzled. Although perhaps she should have guessed by the choice of rainbow trout for the main course...!

'No—I am,' Sam answered smoothly.

Crys turned to him. 'Then it's your birthday...?' Why not? He must have a birthday at some time, just like everyone else, so why not today?

'No, actually it's mine,' interjected a smoothly urbane male voice.

Crys glanced past Molly and Sam to look at the couple who accompanied them: a tall, handsome man, with a woman at his side who was extremely beautiful.

'Matthew Wyngard.' The man smiled as he held out his hand to Crys, his handshake warm. 'And this is my wife, Caroline.' He turned to the woman at his side.

Caroline…!

Crys stared at the woman, who was probably in her late forties or early fifties, with a beauty that was eternal. It would be too much of a coincidence if she wasn't the woman who had telephoned Sam in Yorkshire!

Crys felt a terrible sick feeling in the pit of her stomach as a terrible thought occurred to her—something that, in view of Molly's explanation concerning her relationship to Sam, perhaps should have occurred to Crys before…!

'Say hello, Crystal,' Sam suggested teasingly, although one glance in his direction showed that the expression in his eyes in no way reflected that lightness of manner.

She drew in a deep breath. 'Good evening, Mrs Wyngard,' she greeted tautly, briefly touching the other woman's hand. 'Well, as you can see, all your guests have arrived.' She turned with a sweep of her arm that encompassed the twenty guests already seated at the table. 'Although there still appears to be one missing,' she realised with a frown at the five empty chairs.

It was surprising she could function at all after the shock she had just received! First Molly. And then Sam. Now the introduction to Matthew and Caroline

Wyngard. She was so confused it was a wonder she wasn't burbling incoherently!

Or maybe she was…?

'No one is missing, Crystal,' Sam assured her, standing much closer to her than was comfortable, the older couple having moved off to greet some of the other guests now.

Although Crys now knew that just having Sam in the same room as her would be too close for comfort—her comfort!

'But—'

'The extra setting is for you,' he told her quietly. 'When you're free to join us, of course,' he added, with an understanding look at her heated face.

'Me?' she repeated.

'You,' Sam confirmed. 'Think you can handle it?'

Handle what? At the moment she just felt as if she had completely lost the plot!

'It's really very kind of you,' she answered carefully. 'But I'm afraid—'

'My father has been looking forward to meeting you since we told him earlier that we were giving him a surprise birthday party at your restaurant,' Sam cut in evenly. 'You aren't going to disappoint him, I hope?' he queried in a steely voice.

She blinked. Her worst nightmare was suddenly coming true. Matthew *was* Sam's father. Which meant that Caroline was Molly's mother. Sam's *stepmother*!

'Matthew,' Sam explained. 'And Molly's mother—Caroline,' he continued, frowning at Crys's obvious discomfort. 'Although we always refer to them collectively as "the parents",' he elaborated with obvious affection.

She needed a few minutes to herself to sort herself out, Crys decided, feeling dizzy from the shock of seeing Sam again without the addition of all these other complications!

'I see,' she offered limply. 'Well, if you would like to take your seats at the table, I'll see to the serving of the first course.' That's it, stick to business matters, Crys, she told herself firmly; she knew what she was doing on that level! 'And if I have time I'll join you later,' she added as she saw Sam was about to protest.

'Very well,' he accepted coolly. 'Molly?' He held his arm out for her to accompany him.

'I hope you'll forgive us for the subterfuge,' Molly said to Crys. 'We did so want to surprise Matthew this evening. Booking the table in the name of Gardener was only a little harmless fun on our part.' She chuckled.

But whose idea had it been? Crys wondered with a narrow-eyed look in Sam's direction. Molly's or Sam's? Because the person who had been most surprised this evening was definitely Crys!

'I did think you might guess when I ordered the trout,' Molly confided.

Perhaps she should have done, Crys admonished herself yet again. She just hadn't given it a thought at the time.

'That was Sam's choice, of course,' Molly elaborated with an affectionate grin in his direction.

Of course it was, Crys knew, deliberately not looking at him. Had it been his idea to have the yellow roses—James's flower—in the centre of the table, too…?

'Do try and join us later, won't you, Crys?' Molly encouraged warmly, before turning to link her arm with Sam's, and strolling over to take their seats at the already crowded table.

Crys watched them go, wondering why it was that she always felt as if she had been put through a meat grinder every time she spent any length of time in Sam Wyngard's company!

Although she did finally seem to have sorted out all the complicated relationships in her mind! And one thing was blazingly obvious—Caroline was not the woman in Sam's life.

But Crys ached to be…!

CHAPTER FOURTEEN

'Isn't that Sam Wyngard out there?' Gerry frowned as he came through to the kitchen some time later.

'It certainly is.' Crys, capably wrestling with the last of the trout to be served as the main course for the twenty-five, gave a hurried confirmation.

'I haven't seen him for years,' Gerry said appreciatively. 'He used to come into Scottie's a lot,' he explained, referring to the restaurant he had managed before coming to work for Crys five years ago. 'A really decent chap. I always thought he got a raw deal years ago over the attempted suicide of that actress he was engaged to. The press literally ripped him to shreds at the time. Nice to see— Whoops.' He stepped forward to move the plate slightly so that Crys didn't drop the trout onto the floor. 'Everything okay, Crys?' He looked at her concernedly.

No, everything was not okay. She still felt completely foolish over her confusion concerning Caroline's relationship to Sam. And now Gerry, it seemed, knew Sam from years ago and thought him a really decent chap!

Who was the real Sam Wyngard? The monster the press had made him out to be ten years ago? Or the loving stepbrother to Molly, caring son to his father and his stepmother, the tender lover he had been to Crys?

She knew without a doubt which person she wanted him to be!

She straightened to take off her apron, placing it decisively back on the rail before smoothing down her black sheath dress and turning to pick up the last plate of trout. 'I've been invited to join the birthday party, Gerry; do you think you and the staff can manage the desserts on your own?'

If Gerry was surprised, then he didn't show it. 'Of course,' he replied. 'Enjoy yourself,' he encouraged as she turned to enter the restaurant.

Crys braced her shoulders once out of the kitchen, drawing in a deeply controlling breath before crossing the room to where the Wyngard family and their guests were obviously having a good time. The conversation—and champagne!—flowed freely.

Having been kept busy in the kitchen for the last hour, Crys had no idea exactly where the empty seat was until she actually reached the table and saw that, because of the odd number of women to men, it was situated between Sam and his stepmother Caroline.

Thank goodness she had never been stupid enough to make any comments to Sam about Caroline—that would have been just too embarrassing.

She felt even worse concerning her earlier assumptions as Caroline turned to smile warmly when Crys sat down in the chair next to her.

'It's so good to meet you at last, my dear.' Caroline reached out and lightly touched her hand in welcome. 'Molly has talked about you for years!'

'And all of you,' Crys returned, very conscious that Sam was seated to her left.

'Really?' he murmured softly in Crys's ear as Caroline's attention was distracted by her husband. 'You didn't look overly pleased when my father made the introductions earlier.'

Crys turned sharply. 'That was because—' She broke off, biting her bottom lip. How could she possibly say it had been because until that moment she had been under the impression that the woman she only knew as 'Caroline' was involved in some sort of relationship with Sam? How could she possibly have known it was his stepmother?

'Because...?' Sam pressed, one dark brow raised sardonically.

'I was surprised to see any of you,' Crys defended. 'And just whose idea *was* that to surprise me as much as your father?'

'Mine, of course,' Sam confessed unabashedly, looking more relaxed this evening than Crys had so far seen him.

'I thought it might have been.'

'Did you? Why?'

'It seemed like something you would do,' Crys ventured, feeling a little shy in his company after the strained way they had parted in Yorkshire. 'Sam, when we last saw each other—'

'Later, Crystal.' He cut across her, one of his hands briefly touching hers to take the sting out of his interruption. 'I'm taking you home when this evening is over. We can talk then.'

'You are?' Crys blinked her surprise, quickly doing an inventory inside her head of just how her apartment had looked when she'd left it earlier today. She was usually a tidy person, and the apartment had been neat and clean when she left. But even so—

'I am,' he assured her firmly.

Despite the fact that he was here, in London, enjoying a social evening with his family and friends, he was obviously no less arrogant than he had been four weeks ago, Crys decided. That would have been too much to hope for!

'Close your mouth, Crystal, and eat your trout,' Sam instructed.

She gave him a withering glance. 'Doesn't one cancel out the other?'

'Just eat, woman,' he told her impatiently. 'I've never seen you finish a meal yet, and you're far too thin as it is!'

'Strange as it may seem, I've never particularly enjoyed my own cooking,' she explained, knowing that it was because once she had finished all the preparation and cooking at the restaurant she no longer felt like eating herself.

Sam gave her a considering look. 'Then perhaps it's time someone cooked a few meals for you,' he said.

'It's a nice thought, but—'

'Your evenings aren't free,' he finished knowingly. 'Actually, Crystal, I was suggesting I cook you breakfast,' he added tentatively.

'Breakfast?' she gasped, eyes wide now as she stared at him, heated colour in her cheeks.

He nodded. 'Warm croissants with honey. How does that sound?'

'Wonderful. But—'

'In bed, of course,' he expanded, in what could only be called a honeyed voice.

Crys shook her head, completely flustered now. He was going much too fast for her. How did he jump from taking her home to bringing her breafast in bed in the morning? With relative ease, it seemed!

She stared down at the snowy-white cloth on the table in front of her, no longer able to look at Sam himself. 'Sam, I don't know what impression you formed of me when I was in Yorkshire—'

'We've already been through that, Crystal.' He squeezed her hand reassuringly. 'But we'll talk about it again later,' he declared gently. 'This is, after all, my father's evening,' he reminded her, with an affectionate glance in the older man's direction.

Matthew Wyngard's evening it most certainly was, and the older man was a gracious and charming host at the surprise party organised by his son and stepdaughter. He thanked the pair most profusely when he made his short speech as they all lingered over coffee. No one, it seemed, was in any hurry to end the evening, despite the fact that it was one o'clock in the morning.

Crys had already dismissed all the staff, including Gerry, assuring him that they could clean up tomorrow, in no hurry herself to bring the evening to an end. She was all too conscious of Sam's arm resting across the back of her seat, of the fact that he was taking her home—of the suggestion he would bring her breakfast in bed in the morning!

In fact, by the time she found herself seated next to Sam, being driven home in a dark green sports car, she felt more like a quiveringly naïve wreck than a twenty-six-year-old woman who had been both married and widowed!

'Relax.' Sam reached out briefly to lightly touch her hands as they twisted nervously together in her lap. 'You enjoyed this evening, didn't you?' he queried.

Surprisingly—after what Sam had said to her!—she had, and had enjoyed several conversations with Molly and 'the parents'. But all the time she'd talked to other people she had been aware of that slightly possessive arm lying across the back of her chair...

'Very much,' she assured him. 'You have a very nice family.'

'I think so.'

Crys moistened dry lips. 'Sam, before you say anything else, I—I think I should tell you that I—' Go on, Crys, she instructed herself firmly. 'I may have made a few erroneous assumptions before this evening—'

'Only a few?' Sam questioned sardonically. 'Caroline is a very beautiful woman, isn't she?' he added knowingly.

Crys turned to glare at him, feeling the warmth in her cheeks. He knew, damn it. He knew *exactly* what she had thought concerning—

'I only realised this evening, when the two of you were introduced and you looked so horrified,' Sam interjected lightly into her embarrassed thoughts. 'That over-active imagination been at work again, Crystal?'

When he put it like that...! 'Perhaps,' she conceded. 'But you were deliberately secretive when we were in Yorkshire together—so close-mouthed about everything that you made a clam look positively chatty! I— What is so funny?' she challenged as he began to chuckle.

'You are,' he told her with a rueful shake of his head. 'And I think I should tell you that I've decided my life as a hermit is over,' he added seriously.

She looked at him in the semi-darkness created by the numerous streetlights outside. 'You have?' she said slowly.

'Mmm.' He nodded. 'I sat there alone in Yorkshire,

after you and Molly left, and realised I can't live that life any more—that if you can carry on with your public life after all the blows dealt out to you this last year, I can certainly weather a few strange looks and frankly unfair accusations whenever I choose to appear in public.'

He was referring to Rachel Gibson…

He gave her a sideways glance. 'That's your cue to ask if they *are* unfair?' he told her.

Maybe it was, but Crys knew with sudden certainty that she didn't need to ask him anything of the sort. Molly obviously adored him. His father and stepmother were obviously incredibly proud of him. Gerry thought he was 'a really decent chap'. And Crys knew she couldn't have fallen in love with him if he wasn't all of those things!

'No,' she answered with certainty, shaking her head. 'I don't need to ask that.'

Sam's hands tightened on the steering wheel of the car until his knuckles showed white. 'Crystal, aren't you even going to give me the benefit of the doubt?'

Crys looked at him, realising as she did so that all his self-confidence of earlier—the way he had taken charge, his claim of bringing her breakfast in bed—had been a front, that underneath all that he was as nervous about the outcome of their conversation as she was!

'Sam…!' she cried achingly, reaching out to lightly clasp his arm, easily able to feel the tension in his body beneath the urbane covering of his evening suit.

The car swerved slightly as Sam reacted to her touch, his expression grim as he glanced at her after straightening the wheel. 'Perhaps we had better leave this until I've at least got us both safely back home,' he suggested. 'I wouldn't like to be accused of being responsible for trying to kill yet another—'

'Sam, don't even say that!' Crys cut in forcefully, knowing exactly what he was going to say. 'I don't believe for a moment all those things Rachel Gibson said about you ten years ago!'

He looked stunned by the claim. 'You don't…?'

'Certainly not,' she assured him firmly. 'Although you could be responsible for my death if you don't soon stop this car and kiss me!' she declared, having been pushed beyond endurance this evening, knowing that all she wanted now was the sweet oblivion of Sam's kisses.

A nerve began to pulse in his cheek; his hands tightly gripped the steering-wheel, and there was a pallor to his cheeks as he glanced at Crys. 'I— You—' He swallowed hard.

'I don't believe it—a dumbstruck Sam Wyngard!' Crys said gleefully, her eyes glowing with laughter. 'I never thought I would see the day…!'

'You, young lady, are going to get your bottom very firmly spanked!' he ground out, even as he drove his car expertly into the underground car park beneath the building where Crys had her apartment.

Crys laughed. 'I'm not even going to ask how you knew where I live, because I know it will have been from Molly,' she said, turning to get out of the car, but stopped from doing so by Sam's hand reaching out and tightly grasping her arm. She turned back to him enquiringly, all her humour fading as she saw the look of uncertainty on his face. 'Oh, Sam…!' She moved across the seat to put her arms about him, her face buried against his shoulder. 'It will be all right,' she comforted. 'You'll see.'

His body began to shake beneath her hands, causing her to burrow all the closer against him in an effort to reassure him.

Until she realised he wasn't shaking because he was upset but because he was laughing!

She raised her head to look at him accusingly. 'What is so funny?'

Sam shook his head, eyes still brimming with laughter. 'I thought it was the man who was supposed to reassure the woman about everything being all right,' he explained in a choked voice, obviously making a great effort to control his laughter.

Crys's own snort of laughter was completely involuntary. 'Let's go upstairs,' she said.

'Best invitation I've had all evening,' Sam accepted, as he followed her out of the car.

Crys had no idea what Fred, the night watchman at the apartment building, thought as she strolled in with Sam at her side. She merely gave the elderly man a smile and a friendly wave before stepping into the lift and pressing the button for her floor.

'Your reputation will be in shreds by this time tomorrow,' Sam observed.

Crys shrugged. 'My mother always said that what people didn't know about you they would make up, anyway, so it's best to just live your life to your own expectations. I've found it's worked so far,' she explained.

Her apartment was as neat and tidy as she had thought it was, light and airy, the yellow and cream décor giving it a welcomingly sunny appearance even in the depths of winter. Which was exactly how James had wanted it to feel when he designed it...

'The yellow roses on the table this evening,' she

blurted out after placing her bag down on the coffee table. 'Why did you choose them? You *did* choose them, didn't you?' she asked uncertainly.

She felt a little awkward now that she and Sam were actually in her apartment. On the drive here, outside, anything had seemed possible. But here, and now... What did Sam really want from her?

Sam looked at her hard. 'You're jumping two steps ahead of where we should start talking,' he said, green gaze intent on her face. 'I've missed you this last month, Crystal,' he told her gruffly.

She swallowed hard before moistening suddenly dry lips. 'I was only there for two days,' she parried. 'And I'm forgetting my manners,' she continued in a self-conscious rush. 'I haven't even offered you a drink—'

'I don't want a drink,' he cut in firmly.

'Fine,' she accepted with an attempt at a smile. 'I— What have you done with Merlin this evening?' she prompted conversationally.

This was awful! What on earth was wrong with her? Downstairs she and Sam had seemed perfectly comfortable with each other, had even laughed together, and yet now—

'He's at the parents' house,' Sam said. 'I thought it best until I find somewhere permanent of my own to live in London.'

Crys gave him a startled look. 'I know you said earlier— You're actually coming back to live in London?' Her heart leapt at the thought of him being closer to her.

'I am,' Sam confirmed, his gaze still fixed intently on her face. 'Not all the time, of course,' he went on.

'I love Yorkshire far too much to do that. But maybe during the week…'

'That will be nice,' Crys responded politely.

'Will it?' Sam's eyes became guarded.

'Of course. You'll be able to see more of your family, and—'

'And you?' he put in.

Crys felt suddenly shy again. 'If you would like to,' she agreed.

He drew in a sharp breath. 'Oh, I would like to. Very much,' he concluded forcefully.

She hesitated briefly. 'I— Are you sure I can't get you a drink? Coffee? Or something?'

Sam shook his head. 'Crystal, I need to tell you what happened ten years ago—'

'Of course you don't,' Crys objected. 'I've already told you I don't believe for one moment that you were responsible for what Rachel did.'

'You didn't feel that way when you left Yorkshire,' he said slowly.

'How can you possibly know what I felt when I left Yorkshire?' Crys's awkwardness began to fade as indignation began to take its place. 'I was under a certain amount of misapprehensions at the time, admittedly,' she conceded. 'But believing you were guilty of the behaviour your fiancée claimed—'

'Ex-fiancée,' Sam interrupted. 'That was the problem!'

'Whatever,' Crys agreed. 'That certainly wasn't one of them. Sam, I didn't leave because I had realised who you were and why you had lived alone in the wilds of Yorkshire for ten years,' she stated firmly.

He looked totally perplexed. 'Then why did you

leave so suddenly? And don't tell me it was because the restaurant was busy, because I won't believe you.'

'Ah.' There was no way she could just blurt out that she had left because she had realised she was in love with him—and the emotion terrified the life out of her. At least…it had then. This last four weeks without even seeing him had shown her that she might try to run away from love, but it refused to go away! Just looking at Sam now, she knew she loved him more than ever.

'Ah?' Sam prompted softly.

'Hmm.' She pulled a face. 'Sam, in the last year I've lost not only my husband, but also my parents—'

'I know!' he exclaimed, suddenly moving towards her. 'It must have been awful for you. I can't even begin to imagine…! Maybe I can,' he amended. 'Crystal, earlier you said that if I didn't soon kiss you you were going to die—well, if I don't soon kiss you I think I might just do the same thing!' He groaned before his arms moved about her possessively and his mouth claimed hers.

Crys returned his kiss with all the pent-up love inside her, her body moulded against his, her arms up over his shoulders as she strained to be even closer still.

Sam broke the kiss suddenly, resting the dampness of his forehead against her. 'I love you, Crystal. I love you so much!' he declared. 'This last four weeks without seeing you has been hell—much worse than anything I've ever known in my life before.'

Worse than realising his fiancée was possessively jealous to the point of instability. Worse than feeling in part responsible when she attempted to take her own life. Worse than the pain and loneliness he had suffered during the ten years since that time.

They had both suffered, it seemed, in their different ways. But through that pain they had somehow managed to fall in love with each other.

'Oh, Sam, I love you, too,' she choked emotionally.

He drew in a sharp breath. 'Enough to marry me?'

'Oh, yes!' She had no doubts, no questions to ask about anything—knew that she was loved as much as she loved.

'The yellow roses on the table tonight.' He gruffly answered the question she had asked him earlier. 'I wanted you to know that I accept how much you loved James, that if I can ever persuade you into loving me in return, I would never try to take any of that away from you.' His hands reached up to cradle each side of her face. 'Do you understand?'

She did understand. She understood that Sam realised she hadn't loved James more, or less, than she now loved him, only that it had been different from the love the two of them now shared.

It was enough. More than enough!

'There, that wasn't so bad, was it?' Crys cajoled as Sam resumed his seat next to hers, the sound of the applause continuing long after he had sat down.

Sam looked down at the award he held in his hand for best screenwriter—the sixth for this *Bailey* series. Only this year Sam had appeared in person to collect his award. Something the audience were obviously very appreciative of.

They had been married just over a year now—a year during which they had alternated between living in the house in London they had bought, and Falcon

House in Yorkshire. It had been the happiest year of Crys's life—a year when she had seen Sam returned to his former personal popularity. The *Bailey* series was growing ever more successful, and several directors had approached him from America about writing screenplays for them now that he was no longer a recluse.

'No, it wasn't so bad,' Sam conceded. 'But wait until it's your turn to go up and collect your award, and see how you feel,' he teased.

Crys's cookery programme had been nominated for an award of its own. 'I already have my award,' she told him softly, her smile enigmatic.

Sam gave a puzzled frown. 'You're smiling that smile again...'

Crys leant forward and whispered softly in his ear before leaning back into her own seat, her eyes glowing with happiness as she looked at him.

He swallowed hard. 'Are you sure?'

'Positive,' she assured him smugly.

The whoop of joy he gave as he lifted her up out of her seat and into his arms caused many heads to turn their way, but they were completely impervious to those stares as they shared a kiss of complete happiness.

Their son, or daughter, would be born before the end of the year.

MILLS & BOON

Summer of
LOVE

CANDY HALLIDAY
HOLLY JACOBS
CATHIE LINZ
ELISE TITLE

Available from 16th May 2003

*Available at most branches of WH Smith,
Tesco, Martins, Borders, Eason, Sainsbury's
and all good paperback bookshops.*

0603/49/MB75

2 Books
and a surprise gift!

We would like to take this opportunity to thank you for reading this Mills & Boon® book by offering you the chance to take TWO more specially selected titles from the Modern Romance™ series absolutely FREE! We're also making this offer to introduce you to the benefits of the Reader Service™—

- ★ FREE home delivery
- ★ FREE gifts and competitions
- ★ FREE monthly Newsletter
- ★ Books available before they're in the shops
- ★ Exclusive Reader Service discount

Accepting these FREE books and gift places you under no obligation to buy; you may cancel at any time, even after receiving your free shipment. Simply complete your details below and return the entire page to the address below. *You don't even need a stamp!*

YES! Please send me 2 free Modern Romance books and a surprise gift. I understand that unless you hear from me, I will receive 4 superb new titles every month for just £2.60 each, postage and packing free. I am under no obligation to purchase any books and may cancel my subscription at any time. The free books and gift will be mine to keep in any case.

P3ZEB

Ms/Mrs/Miss/Mr ....Initials.............................
BLOCK CAPITALS PLEASE

Surname...

Address...

....

....Postcode ....

Send this whole page to:
UK: The Reader Service, FREEPOST CN81, Croydon, CR9 3WZ
EIRE: The Reader Service, PO Box 4546, Kilcock, County Kildare (stamp required)

Offer not valid to current Reader Service subscribers to this series. We reserve the right to refuse an application and applicants must be aged 18 years or over. Only one application per household. Terms and prices subject to change without notice. Offer expires 29th August 2003. As a result of this application, you may receive offers from Harlequin Mills & Boon and other carefully selected companies. If you would prefer not to share in this opportunity please write to The Data Manager at the address above.

Mills & Boon® is a registered trademark owned by Harlequin Mills & Boon Limited.
Modern Romance™ is being used as a trademark.